Eight Days

A Love Always Novella

d. Nichole King

Eight Days

Limitless Publishing, LLC
Kailua, HI 96734
www.limitlesspublishing.com

Formatting: Limitless Publishing

ISBN-13: 978-1-68058-193-5
ISBN-10: 1-68058-193-7

Dedication

For all those who fell in love
with Kate and Damian's story.
For all those who found
a little piece of comfort through it.
For all those who have shared your stories with me.
For all those who asked for more of Damian.
Readers, this is for you.

Midnight

Damian

I know hospital protocol, but I refuse to sit in a waiting room full of depressed people hoping a doctor will come out of the ER with good news. It's never good. Not in a hospital.

I don't go home, though. I need to know as soon as I can what's wrong with Kate.

What's this girl doing to me? I'm about to lose my goddamn mind.

As soon as I've closed the door to Dad's office, I go directly for his desk. I drop to my hands and knees and reach to the back of the bottom drawer. When I feel the hard plastic case, I rip it off and dump the key in my palm. Just hearing the click of the drawer's lock soothes me a little.

A picture of Mom stares up at me and makes me pause. Her eyes remind me of Kate's—kind and compassionate. She's laughing, blonde hair falling in her face. I know this picture. It's the day she found out she was pregnant with my brother, Liam.

I turn the frame over so she doesn't see what I really want in Dad's drawer. My fingers close around the silver flask. I lift it out and slam the drawer closed. Unscrewing the cap, I sit in the doc's chair with my feet on the desk, the way he hates.

I tip the flask back, letting the whiskey burn away the sting in my chest. It's all too familiar, and I won't let it consume me again. I drown the feeling out with another gulp. Then another until nothing is left.

But my chest still hurts.

Kate's file is under my heels. I lower my legs and pick it up, opening the flimsy cover. The fucking thing is so thick a lump rises in my throat at the weight of it. Last time I'd only flipped through it to find out who she was; this time I'll read every damn word.

I start in the back of the file, when she'd gone in for what her doctors thought was mono. I don't care that I don't understand half the shit in here; it still hurts like hell to read everything she's been through.

The further into the file I venture, the more I realize that being with Kate is incredibly stupid. She's sick, and I could lose her at any second. I know the deeper I go with her, the harder it will be to walk away. And I *should* walk away.

I'm not good for her, and she's not good for me.

She needs someone other than me. Someone stronger, who won't fall apart when shit gets real. That's my MO. Even tonight, if the news is bad, I don't think I can handle it. I'm a fucked-up mess.

Halfway through, I shut the file and push it as far from me as possible. The thing almost falls off the desk.

"I'm done. I can't do this," I mutter, digging my phone out of my back pocket. I need to cut ties with Kate before I'm too attached.

I dial the number to the one girl who's good at numbing my mind. She picks right up like she always does. Tonight, I need her as much as *she* usually needs *me*.

"Hey!" Ellie says, chipper for this late. She's been waiting for me to call; I hear it in her voice. "Want some company?"

"Yeah, but I'm at the hospital. Meet me here?"

"Why're you at the hospital?"

"I'm working late."

Ellie sighs. "Okay, whatever. I'll be right over."

I hang up and head to the elevators. It's a short trek from Drake University, and I need to meet her outside because we've never hooked up here before.

Out in the parking lot, I make my way to my car and slide inside. I grab the package of cigarettes from the console. I don't know what everyone else who works here does, but it's my car and I'll smoke in it if I damn well please.

I light up and watch the cars turning into the parking lot. There's not many at 3 a.m. I blow out the smoke. Damn, this shit is relaxing.

When I see Ellie's car, I open my door and toss the butt. I didn't bring a jacket, and the chill bites. It's not a big deal, though, and I walk to where she's parking her ten year old Intrepid.

"I thought you said you were working?" she

says, eyeing me.

I peer down at my shirt and jeans. "It's the middle of the night, Elle. No uniforms needed."

She shrugs. "Whatevs. Are we going inside? It's freezing out here."

"Yeah," I say and take her hand, leading her toward the main entrance.

I guide her into the elevator as fast as I can. The last thing I need is for Kate's parents to see me with Ellie. Or maybe that's the only thing I need. Letting go of Kate would be easier that way.

I don't know.

"What's going on, Damian?" Ellie asks as soon as the doors close. "You're acting weird. I mean, we don't have to—"

"Nothing, Ellie. I'm fine," I say calmly.

I'm anything but fine.

We step off on the third floor—the pediatric oncology floor—the one I know best. There's a string of empty rooms on the other side of the nurses' station, and no one enters them unless a patient occupies one.

I pull Ellie behind me to the farthest room. Taking a quick glance around for hospital staff, I open the door when I confirm there's no one around.

"Come on," I say.

Ellie's eyes narrow as she takes in the door. "Is there a lock?"

"No," I reply, shutting the door and sliding the curtain closed inside the room.

"Uh, maybe we shouldn't…"

"Shhh." I grip her hips and press them into me.

Damn, I already ache to be inside her. "Don't worry. Nobody comes in here."

I lower my head to suck on her neck. Over my shoulder, I feel her staring at the closed door, waiting for an interruption I know won't come. She's not usually like this, and it's starting to piss me off. I need her, and I need her now. I decide to move things along, loosen her up a bit.

I spin her around against the bed. "Face forward," I tell her, and I lift her arms over her head. She tries to sneak a peek at me after I have her t-shirt off, but I gently push her head back where I want it.

"Elle." I breathe her name into her ear, and she relaxes a little. Unfortunately, it's not enough. Her muscles are still too tense. "Come on, baby. Work with me, here."

"Damian, the door—"

"I said don't worry about it." Somehow, I need to get her mind off that damn door.

I don't bother with her bra; I go straight for her jeans. Her palms settle on the backs of my hands as I unbutton and unzip them. Latching my thumbs into her panties too, I lower myself to the floor along with her bottoms. She steps out of them, and I toss them somewhere. On the cold tile, I position myself behind her. Between those long legs.

"Oh!" she gasps, understanding my intentions to relax her. She leans forward over the edge of the bed. The fun is about to begin.

I spread her lips apart and let my tongue work over her. She's not wet, but it doesn't take long before she's rocking against me. I fucking love when she moves her hips on my face like this.

Other than Ellie's uneven breaths and low moans, the room is quiet. Too quiet, and from the hallway, I hear the hospital intercom: "Dr. Lowell to emergency, please. Dr. Lowell to emergency."

Kate. It has to be Kate.

"Damian? Why did you stop?" Ellie whines, breathless. I hadn't realized I'd quit licking her.

No, I remind myself. *I'm letting go before it's too late.*

Pushing thoughts of Kate out of my head, I grin and run two fingers from Ellie's front all the way to the back. She shudders.

"I'm not," I say. "Just warming up."

Jumping to my feet, I strip down quickly. I need to be inside this girl pronto. She smiles at me over her shoulder, no longer preoccupied with the unlocked door.

"Nope," I tell her when her gaze meets mine.

It's no longer about the door; it's about something I can control. She bites her lip and obeys, turning her head around again. I glide both of my hands over her ass and up her back, pushing her chest forward onto the bed.

She giggles in anticipation, whipping her long, blonde curls over one shoulder. It's the sexiest thing she's done so far tonight. I push up behind her, teasing her at first. Ellie pouts, letting out a little girly whimper. I can't keep her waiting, so I oblige, entering her with a deep thrust.

"Oh, yes!" she squeals, and I wish I could see her face, her mouth open in sheer pleasure.

The door has been completely forgotten. All she

feels is me.

I pump into her, her fluids coating me with warmth. Unbidden, I think about sitting in front of the fireplace with Kate in the den. I'd gotten too involved that night, and now I need to reverse it.

I have to move on, away from Kate. I've got to get her out of my mind.

Ellie's moans grow louder, and each time I pound into her, I repeat "move on" in my head.

"I. Can't. Hold. On," Ellie pants before she buries her face in the blankets and screams out her satisfaction.

I thrust into her a few more times, deeper and deeper until I shove myself in as far as I can and let out a deep groan. Ellie's still breathing into the mattress when I pull out and fall on the bed beside her.

Moving. On.

~*~

I throw on my clothes with Ellie's gaze hard on my back. Tossing my shirt over my head, I spin around to face her. "What?"

She sits on the bed, her legs dangling over the edge. "You're not working tonight," she states, peering up at me through long lashes.

I shrug. "So?"

"Then why here?" Her voice cracks a little, and I wonder if she's thinking of my brother and how, at my house, she feels closer to him even though she's fucking me. Maybe that thought makes what we do easier for her.

"Because this is where I was tonight," I say, slipping into my shoes.

"You hate being here."

I button up my shirt, ignoring her. I don't appreciate her giving me the third degree.

"Does this have to do with the girl you were with last night?" Ellie asks.

I about piss myself. How the hell does she know about Kate?

"What girl?"

Ellie shifts nervously on the bed. "I, uh, ran into your dad and he said you were having dinner with some girl."

Some girl?

I puff out a laugh. If that's all she knows, it's no big deal. Hell, I'm not sure why it's a big deal if she knows anyway. "What, are you jealous or something?"

She hesitates, her eyes wandering around the room, never landing on me. "Of course not. You're free to…do whatever you want."

I have no idea where she's going with this conversation.

She slides off the bed. "Liam would have—"

Oh, that's what this is about.

I yank back the curtain too hard. I hate when she compares the two of us, when anyone does. "I don't want to discuss Liam, all right? He's dead. He's not coming back. Get over it."

Ellie grabs her purse, looking like she might cry. I was a little harsh, but damn, it's been two years since he died.

"Fine," she rasps out. "I'll see myself out."

"Call you later," I say, but she doesn't answer.

~*~

I make my way back to Dad's office. Kate has crept back into my mind, and I feel obligated to find out how she's doing before I leave. It *was* my phone call that brought her here in the first place. A few hours ago, I'd been sitting by her side in her bedroom watching as she gasped for air. Scariest shit I've ever seen.

Her file is still on the desk. As I walk past, I pick it up, rescuing it from falling to the floor. I dump it back in the middle and try to ignore it, but I can't. It draws me in. Going back to where I left off, I begin to read again.

I'm so engrossed that I don't hear my dad come in.

"Patient information is confidential," he says, and I jerk my head up.

"I'm not the one who left it out for the world to see," I retort. "How is she?"

Dad sinks down in a chair opposite me, where his patients usually sit. Kate and her parents have probably sat there many times.

"She's checked in to a room now." He takes off his glasses and places them gently on the desk.

"That's not what I asked."

"You know I can't discuss this with you, Damian. You're not family. What's going on between you two, anyway?"

I stand up and shoot him a sly smile. "You know I can't discuss this with you." I walk past him, toward the door. "Confidential. You understand."

Asshole.

I see Tammy at the nurses' station. She kinda likes me, I think. Worth a shot.

"What room is Kate Browdy in?" I ask, leaning against the counter.

She looks up from the computer and a genuine smile spreads across her face. "It's past visiting hours, Damian, and—"

"My shift starts in five hours, Tammy. I'm gonna find out, so you may as well tell me now." I'm being a dick. Sure, it annoys me that she's dancing around the issue, but to have any shot at getting the three numbers out of her, I need to watch my tone. I grin, hoping the dimples Kate stares at all the time work on nurses too.

Apparently they do.

Tammy sighs. "310. Her parents are with her now."

"Perfect. Thanks, Tammy."

Room 310 is only a dozen steps away, the door cracked open. I knock softly and enter even though I haven't been invited. Before bowing out of her life, I need to know she'll be okay.

Two sets of eyes swing in my direction, but I don't see them. I only see her. IVs stick out of her hands, tubes poke into her, and cords hooked up to machines surround the bed. Her eyelids are closed, and some hose is doing the breathing for her.

I stand frozen, unable to rip my gaze away. Something in my chest makes it hard to suck in air. She looks so fragile, like she could break at any second. Shatter into a million pieces.

And all I want to do is hold her. Sweep her up in my arms and never let go.

Guilt swells inside me, and my heart literally hurts. An hour ago I was screwing Ellie and trying to convince myself that I needed to back out of Kate's life. I'm a fucking asshole.

"Damian." Marcy stands up, wiping tears from her cheeks.

"What's going on? Is Kate okay?" I barely get the words out.

"It's viral," Marcy croaks out, her voice breaking. "It, uh, has to run its course, but Kate…she, um, her immune system can't fight it because she's so weak from the chemo."

The medication that's supposed to kill the cancer is making it so she can't fight off normal viral shit?

"So, what does that mean?" I ask, confused.

Marcy swipes away another tear. If Marcy is crying, this thing is bad. Real bad. "Dr. Lowell— your dad—put her in a medicated coma."

What the fuck?

"She has to fight through this. Putting her under means her body only has to concentrate on one thing: killing the virus," Marcy explains.

I don't fully comprehend. What hits me, though, is that she might not pull through this. The virus could kill her, and I'm pretty sure I won't be able to handle that.

I nod toward Kate. "Can I?"

Marcy offers a slight smile. "She'd want you to."

In slow motion, I walk around the foot of the bed, studying her. Her chest rises and falls, and I hold my breath for a second, waiting for the next rise. I can't help but wonder how many more times I'll see that happen.

I lower myself into a chair opposite Mr. Browdy. He's holding Kate's hand to his lips like he won't let go until she opens her eyes again. I get that because it's how I feel at the moment too.

He glances up at me as I take Kate's other hand. I meet his gaze, but I can't read it. Right now, I don't really give a fuck if he doesn't approve of me being here. Kate's all that matters.

I kiss her fingers. They feel so good against my lips, and I know Kate's drawing me to her again. I don't know how she does it.

The thought that I'm already in too deep comes to me. There's no walking away.

Day 1

I don't remember falling asleep, but when I wake up, I have Kate's hand folded in mine. Mr. Browdy is gone, and Marcy is in the corner reading what looks like a medical textbook. Three more are stacked beside her on the floor. The machines buzzing in my ears remind me of reality: Kate's in a coma fighting for her life.

Marcy seems pretty engrossed in the book, and last night she assured me that Kate could still hear us in her medicated state. I doubt it.

"Hey there," I say to her anyway, and honestly I feel like a shithead. My late night hour with Ellie reels through my mind, and I automatically wipe a palm across my mouth. "I'm sorry, Kate."

I'm not sure exactly what I'm apologizing for. Fucking Ellie? Fucking Ellie while I should have been with her? Or that Kate is even here in the first place?

I want to tell her I won't leave her, but I can't promise that. She deserves better than me. And I deserve…

I think of Liam's disgusted glare when he walked out of our house the last time—how I was supposed to be the one who went with Mom that evening.

…to be where Kate is. It should be me.

"I take it you're not helping out today?" Tammy asks, walking in with a chart and pulling me out of the memory.

"I will in here."

The nurse smiles at me, approving what I said.

Marcy peeks up from her book but doesn't say anything. Standard hospital procedures are probably old hat for her.

Tammy studies the print out from one of the machines and checks Kate's IV. "Behind you, Damian: can you read me her blood pressure numbers?"

I twist around and peer at the monitor. "Uh, one ten over seventy-five." Whatever that means.

Tammy makes a face and jots the numbers down, sighing. "All right, I'll be back in an hour," she says to Marcy. "Dr. Lowell should be making rounds soon."

"Thank you, Tammy." Marcy lays her book on her lap and rubs her temples. "I'm going to the cafeteria for some lunch. You should grab something to eat too," she tells me.

I nod. "When you get back. That way Kate's not alone." The words roll off my tongue, and it takes me a second to realize that I'd actually said them.

I think I see a tear glistening in Kate's mother's eye when she grins at me. "Okay. I won't be long."

As soon as she leaves, I stand up and kiss Kate

on the forehead. Her skin feels amazingly soft against my lips, and I take my time withdrawing them. "You can fight this, Katie."

I sink back into the chair and take her hand, gliding my thumb over the pale skin. Kate's a proven warrior, and I believe in her. She's stronger than anyone I know.

And that's the hitch.

I throw a glance at the door and immediately consider making an escape. Unlike Kate, I'm not strong. Holding onto her, letting her inside, is fucked up. More fucked up than cutting my losses and getting the hell out.

But she already has me. Somehow, Kate lured me in.

Suddenly it hits me that losing her on my terms is less scary than the alternative. But even that doesn't scare the shit out of me as much as realizing that I care about her. It's fucking suicide.

What is it about this girl that has me sitting here, hoping to God she'll wake up and smile at me again?

I slide two fingers down her cheek and over her lips. She doesn't flinch, and it's as if she can't feel me. Something jabs into the pit of my stomach. I'd give anything to hear her voice right now. The sweet naïveté she wears is gorgeous on her, and for whatever the reason, makes me want to protect her from the world's monsters. Monsters like me.

Except, I can't do a damn thing about the monster that's killing her.

I can't save her.

~*~

"Okay, I'm back. You go," Marcy says when she comes in.

"Yeah," I agree. "I'm gonna run home, I think."

"Has your dad been in yet?"

"No." *Thank God.* "I'm sure he will be soon."

On my way out, I run into Leslie. I know I'm on her shit list, but I couldn't care less. I'm not volunteering at this godforsaken hospital by choice, and I've made that perfectly clear to my father and his precious staff.

This nurse, though, hates me more than the others; she remembers my brother.

"How's Kate?" she asks.

The question strikes me as odd. What am I supposed to say? The truth? Well, the fucking truth is that she's so goddamn sick that my dad knocked her out, and she may never wake up. But hey, Leslie knows that.

"Go see for yourself," I scoff and brush past her.

I drive home, and my first stop is the liquor cabinet. Dad keeps it fully stocked even though he's never home and he rarely drinks. I guess he thinks that if he keeps me happy, I'll stay the hell out of his way.

It works.

Not bothering with a glass, I snatch a bottle of Jack and take a long swig. Damn, that's good stuff. I hold the cap in my hand and stare at it. I should twist it back on, gather my stuff, and go back to the hospital, but I don't. Instead, I take another drink and haul it with me to my room.

I'm not sure why I pack a bag of clothes. I just do. I grab my guitar too.

After dropping my shit by the bedroom door, I strip down and stand under the shower. Ellie is still on me, and for the first time in my life, I can't stand it. If I really care about Kate, then what the hell am I doing with Ellie? She's my brother's girlfriend, not mine. *Not mine!*

I press my forehead against the tile. When did life get so fucking complicated?

As the hot water begins to cool, I shut it off and swipe the Jack off the counter. I don't bother with a towel. I sit on the edge of my bed and hold the bottle between my legs. Tapping the neck with one hand, I wipe the other over my face. Then, I gulp down another swash of amber as Liam re-enters my mind.

Suddenly, I'm fifteen again and Liam is with me at the kitchen table, helping me with my chemistry assignment.

"Close, Damian. It's actually tetrahedral; hydrogen can't have a double bond," he says, flipping to the back of the textbook to show me.

"I'm never going to understand this," I say, frustrated.

"You're a sophomore taking senior chem. You can handle this."

I shake my head. "I'm not like you. Or Dad."

Liam grins, but he knows I'm right. I'll never be like either of them. "You don't have to be us. Be yourself."

"Nobody likes me for me. They like me for you."

Liam sighs because he understands. He's overheard the teachers at school. And Dad. He hears Dad all the time. "I never meant to put pressure on you. You know that, right?" Liam says.

"It doesn't matter. I'll always be compared to you."

"Let me talk to Dad. Maybe you can switch schools in the fall, somewhere no one knows me, and you can focus on your music."

"He'll never agree to that, but thanks."

He grips my shoulder and squeezes. "You never know, Damian."

"I know Dad, and I know how the world works. Being like the two of you guarantees I'll be successful someday."

Liam is silent for a moment, his gaze wandering to the sliding glass doors. "Don't be so sure. The world is bigger than you, little brother. Bigger than all of us."

I take another drink to wash away the memory and put the cap back on. I have a buzz going now, though it's not enough to numb my mind. What I really want is to drown myself in the rest of this bottle and another one. Instead, I shake the loose water off my hair and get dressed. Before I leave, I rinse my mouth out with Listerine, getting rid of the whiskey and what's left of Ellie so I can pretend I'm the man Kate deserves.

The man Liam was.

~*~

I drop off my bag and guitar in Dad's office before slipping into Kate's room. Marcy's dozing in the corner where I left her, the giant book almost falling off her lap.

I return to the chair beside Kate's bed. Taking her hand, I clasp the tiny thing between both of mine. Before I say anything, I steal a glance over my shoulder at Marcy to make sure she's still asleep. She is.

"I'm back, baby," I say, pressing it against my lips. "I've been thinking, Katie, and I, uh, I have a compromise for you. A deal, if you'll accept it. You fight this thing and wake up, and I'll do my damnedest to be better. I can't promise I'll be perfect, but I'll sure as fuck try. Just come back to me."

For some reason, fate put her in my life, and since I can't walk away, I'm going to do whatever it takes to figure out why. All I know is if she beats this virus, I'll have my work cut out for me to uphold my end of the bargain.

I study Kate's face. Lifeless and thin, it tears at me. This isn't her.

I think back to when I first met her. She's perceptive, honest, sweet, hopeful, and brave—all the things I'm not. Leukemia is the catalyst that shows the world how wonderful she really is.

I kiss her again. "Come back to me."

~*~

With visiting hours over for the night, I wander into Dad's office. He's not there, and I figure he went home. I check my phone, half-expecting Ellie to have called, but the screen is empty. I'm not sure what to do about her right now.

I fall onto the leather sofa and strum some random chords on my guitar to clear my mind. Whatever I played resonates with me, and I do it again.

I hum out a melody with it this time. Words form on the tip of my tongue, and they flow out of me as I play:

Here I am, hiding,
Writing out my story; tell me it's boring or is it
All the same
Lines with lyrics
Unexpected, will there be a happy ending?
No, I'm not there yet.

I stop playing for a moment. It's not perfect, but it's a start. I jot down the lyrics and keep going until I have something decent. The song has definite potential. Oftentimes, my music tells me more about myself than I ever could.

If only it would speak faster because I don't have a fucking clue what I'm doing.

I sit beside Kate, holding her hand again. The beeping from the machines in the room has dulled with time, and now I barely hear them.

The Browdys are here too, but no one says anything. We just stare droopy-eyed at Kate, waiting for some sign of life.

Dad walks in, his gaze trained on the floor. I tighten my grip on Kate, too scared to hear what I assume he's going to say. He has that expression on his face. The one that's not good.

I can't let go of her.

He clears his throat before he speaks. "I received the results of Kate's tests."

Mr. Browdy puts an arm around his wife and pulls her close. Fear exudes from Marcy as she shakes her head with a hand over her mouth. We all know what's coming.

A familiar knot twists in my chest. Is this really happening?

"The virus was stronger than we expected. I'm sorry, there's nothing more we can do."

I need someone to blame because losing Kate is unfair. She's too young to die, and I can't go through this again. I fight the urge to jump up and beat the shit out of my father. It's his fault. He should have done more. He should have—

I choke back a sob and bury my face into Kate's stomach. "Wake up, Katie. Please, wake up."

Day 2

I jolt awake, sweat dripping into my eyes. I wipe my face with my palms and push them through my hair, shaking the moisture free. Even though daylight creeps into Dad's office, the clock says it's too early for him to be here and too early for visiting hours to have begun.

That won't stop me, though. Screw the nurses and their ridiculous rules. I need to see her now. Need to see that she's breathing.

I pull on a clean t-shirt from my bag and head down the hallway to her room. No one's at the nurses' station to stop me. I might have been able to sweet-talk Tammy, but I doubt it would have worked with the others. They know me too well.

Marcy is probably sound asleep at this hour, so I enter as quietly as I can, careful not to disturb her. I'm right; she lies in the other hospital bed, unmoving.

The machines around Kate's bed hum, and as much as I hate the sound, it's strangely comforting. Even though the monitor signals out a heartbeat, I lean over her, my ear pressing against her chest. I have to hear it for myself, from the source. It thumps softly as her lungs fill with air then deflate. Slow and steady.

I breathe out my relief.

My dream last night; it was only a stupid dream, but damn it felt real. Kate shouldn't have to go through this by herself. As I sit with her now, listening to the beeps and whirls of hospital equipment, I know I won't be crashing in Dad's office another night. Not until she's safe.

Yeah, her mom will stay all night too so she won't be alone, but my decision isn't for Kate. If she slips away and I'm not here, I'll never forgive myself.

I wish I knew how this girl got to me, and what makes me come back for more. Even unconscious she draws me to her. She radiates strength and goodness that calls out to me, taunting me with its power. Telling me it could be mine if I can grasp onto it.

I won't. I can't. I'd just fuck it up.

I run my fingers over her face, letting her warmth sink deep into me. It feels so damn good to be this close to her. "I'm here, baby. I'm not leaving again."

Even as I say it, I wonder if I mean it. Every second I'm with her is another reminder that she's too good for me and I'm a weak son of a bitch who crossed paths with her.

When my fingers trace her lips, I peek over at Marcy. She's still asleep and I smile. I need to feel Kate's lips against mine before everyone's awake.

Maybe she'll wake up.

I kiss her lightly because I don't want to break her. Her mouth is so soft, and I can still taste a faint hint of strawberries lingering from her lip gloss. Damn, I don't want to stop. I suck one of her lips between my teeth, then roll my tongue over the tender skin, allowing her to consume me.

My whole body instantly warms, and I mold my mouth to hers with an urgency I've never owned before. It's scary how much I need this girl.

I break away and stare at her, waiting. After a minute, her lashes don't even flutter.

She doesn't wake up, and I'm powerless to help her.

The day slinks by, and I leave once to gather my shit from Dad's office. Otherwise, I stay by Kate's side the whole time. Marcy brings me food when she goes to the cafeteria. Even though we don't talk much, I think she enjoys my company. She spends her time reading a slew of medical books she borrows from Dad. When she finishes with one, he brings her another. Once in a while, she'll cross-reference something she read on her laptop.

My phone buzzes, but when I notice it's a text from Ellie, I don't read it. I should cut off our arrangement. It's the right thing to do—what *Liam* would do—but I can't.

With Ellie, it's complicated. We have a history, and when we're together, it's like we're keeping a little piece of Liam alive because he belonged to both of us. If I let her go, I'll have to let him go, too. I'm not ready for that.

I stroke Kate's arm; I can't stop touching her. God, I'd give anything to fight this battle for her. She shouldn't have to do this alone.

When Mr. Browdy arrives after work, my dad follows him in. He hasn't spoken to me all day, and that's fine by me. I have nothing to say to him.

"Damian," he says, and I don't bother acknowledging him. "Can I speak with you out in the hall, please?"

Fuck, really?

I kiss Kate's hand. "I'll be right back," I whisper against her skin.

I nod at Mr. Browdy on my way out. Doc is waiting for me at the nurses' station, which I'm relieved to see is empty.

"I see you've cleared your things out of my office," he says, leaning against the counter.

"Yeah, so?"

"Look, Damian, I don't know what you're doing with Kate Browdy, but she isn't Ellie or any of the other girls you bring home at night. This is serious."

"You don't think I know that?" I point to Kate's room, keeping my eyes focused on the asshole in front of me. "Kate is in there fighting for her goddamn life, and what the hell are you doing for her? Aren't you her doctor?"

"I'm letting her fight. It's all I *can* do." He sighs, takes off his glasses, and pinches the bridge of his nose like this conversation exhausts him. "But her illness isn't what I was talking about, Damian."

I understood what he'd asked before. Clearly. I

just didn't have the answer.

"Kate's been through a lot," he continues, "and she has a long road ahead of her. Now, I didn't say anything when you started messing around with Ellie—the two of you can figure it out for yourselves—but you need to think long and hard about your intentions with Kate."

The more he talks the lower his voice drops, his gaze digging into me, and I realize that after seven years of treating her, he's worried about the direction her disease is taking.

"Cancer will always be a part of her life, and the fact is, it may consume her in the end. Kate's different, Damian. Her leukemia makes her different."

From the corner of my eye, I notice Leslie round the edge of the nurses' station. She'll act as if she's minding her own business, but I've been here long enough to know better. All the nurses on this floor know everything that goes on, and it's not because they keep to themselves.

Dad's eyes flick to her, and he slides his glasses back on. "Don't hurt her, son. She deserves better."

I stare at his back as he walks away, and, as much as it pisses me off coming from him, I can't help agreeing with him.

It's getting late, and visiting hours end in fifteen minutes. I have no clue if Marcy will be okay with me staying. Fuck the hospital staff; I don't care what *they* think. All I know is I can't sleep in Dad's office another night, wondering if Kate's okay.

Yet Dad's words stick with me. I shouldn't care about this girl so much. I'll end up hurting her like I hurt everyone else who enters my life.

Mr. Browdy leans over his daughter and kisses her on the forehead. I wonder if I should step out and give them a moment, but I don't because what if one of the nurses catches me and doesn't let me back in? I can't risk that.

"I love you, princess," he tells her. "Hang in there, and I'll see you tomorrow. Your mom and Damian are here if you need anything."

Him mentioning my name like that knocks the breath out of me. We haven't talked much, and even though I know he was grateful for me calling my dad when Kate got sick, I wasn't sure what he thought about me hanging around her room.

He nods at me before taking his wife's hand. "Walk me out?" he asks her.

After they leave, I'm happy to have Kate all to myself for a few minutes. I run my fingertips over her lips before I kiss them. One thing's for sure, I haven't kissed her enough.

"When you wake up, Kate, I swear I'll…" I trail off because I'm not sure how to finish my thought. I'll what? Kiss her forever or just one more time before I run off with my tail between my legs?

I don't have a clue, so I clear my throat and start over.

"When you wake up, Kate, I'll be right here." As of now, that's my plan.

I chew on the inside of my lip, thinking I should say more. Let it all out in case she doesn't wake up.

Problem is, I haven't figured out what "it" is. So, I ramble, hoping to fill in the missing pieces as I go. "You've been asleep for two days now, and I don't have a fucking idea what I'm still doing here, Kate. When I saw you the first time, hooked up to the IV, I wrote you off as another chemo patient I'd see hanging around until you either went into remission or you…"

I don't want to say the rest. I take a deep breath and keep talking. "Then I saw you in the parking lot, and my first thought was how beautiful you were. I couldn't figure out how a girl like you could be throwing up in the parking lot like that. But then I recognized you from the chemo room. The two didn't fit together—the girl outside with the girl with cancer. The girl outside was normal.

"You know, the day we had dinner in the cafeteria, I almost bailed. Even now, I don't know how I ended up in the chemo room with you. Then we got to talking, and I realized that after all you've been through, you still smiled. Still hoped. Cancer didn't take that away from you. That moment I knew how much better you are than me." I feel the corners of my lips tug upward as the memory envelops me. "And how much I loved seeing you smile.

"I know you think you're broken, but you're not. You are so fucking far from being broken, baby. So far. Me on the other hand? Well, I see you and you make *me* less broken."

My gaze wanders over her, and I lean in to kiss her again. How many more kisses I have left I don't know, but I'll enjoy each one until then.

The shifting of clothing alerts me to someone else in the room, and I look up. Leslie is standing in the doorway, her eyebrows perked.

"Don't you knock?" I ask, irritated that she interrupted Kate and me.

"I'm sorry. I saw the Browdys leave, and I assumed she was alone."

"Yeah, well you assumed wrong."

She steps toward the bed. "Damian, what you said—"

Of course she was listening. Nosy bitch.

"What do you want, Leslie?"

She folds her hand over Kate's. "To see her for a minute. That's all." The nurse watches Kate for a few moments. She wears the same expression my father had on earlier: worry. "She'll pull through this. She always does." What she says doesn't match the tone in her voice.

Leslie pats Kate's hand and heads for the door, but suddenly turns around. "Visiting hours are over, by the way."

"Yeah, I know."

She nods once at me before closing the door behind her.

~*~

"It's late, Damian," Marcy says as she digs through her overnight bag. She pulls out a toothbrush and toothpaste in a plastic bag.

"Um, about that. Would you mind if I stayed in here? I can sleep in this chair. I want to be here when she wakes up."

She pauses, contemplating my request. "I'm sure the chair won't be very comfortable."

"Probably not, but I'll make it work."

"Hmm, all right. I'll go ask one of the nightshift nurses for an extra pillow and blanket."

I puff out a sigh of relief. If she said no, I'd have respected that. I wouldn't have liked it, though.

My cell goes off, and I check the text. Another one from Ellie. I stare at the screen before I silence the phone without checking her message. Again. It stings, but I can't deal with Ellie right now, and I sure as hell won't be meeting her tonight for another round of playtime.

No, tonight I'm staying with Kate.

Day 3

When I open my eyes, the first thing I see is Kate, and it's amazing. She has that effect on me. The only thing that could make it better would be waking up next to her outside this goddamn hospital.

I lift my head off the pillow I laid at the edge of her bed sometime in the middle of the night. My muscles are sore, but it's a small price to pay to be this close to her. Marcy's not in the other bed; she's probably in the cafeteria eating breakfast. I'm not hungry yet—well, not for food anyway.

All I want to do is lie in bed with Kate. Have her wrapped inside my arms where nothing can hurt her. I fucking need this girl. I know it's stupid to be with her. The longer I stay, the more entranced I become.

And that scares the piss out of me.

As my gaze wanders over her, I think of how it's a risk I'm willing to take. I don't know why, but I'm beyond caring about the reasons. In fact, all I care about is that Kate wakes up.

I push the pillow to the bottom of the bed, and carefully, I lay myself out on the small sliver of mattress on Kate's side. I move the tubes so I don't stop the flow of chemicals running into her veins. Even though they're supposedly helping her, I want to rip them off. She shouldn't have to depend on this shit to survive.

The machines beep steadily, and I assume I'm in the clear. I haven't fucked anything up. I press my lips on her cheek and keep them there, breathing her in. The sterile scent of latex and bleach sticks to her, but underneath it I can make out her personal aroma. It's something floral, I think. Whatever it is, it's permanently etched into my memory.

"Come on, baby. Pull through this," I whisper in her ear.

The medication is keeping her in the induced coma, and I don't know how long my dad plans on maintaining this spectacle. It's insane.

I glide my fingertips over her jaw, her lips, and down her neck. I can't help pausing to feel her pulse. Actually feeling it thump against my finger is comforting. More so than hearing the stale, mechanic beep of the heart monitor.

"The offer still stands." I'm not sure why I say it, I just do. "I can be better for you, Kate. I *will* be better for you."

My phone goes off, and by the ringtone, I know it's Ellie. I don't know what she wants at this early hour. I haven't checked the text she sent me last night, and even though I'm lying here with Kate, a part of me wants to jump off this bed and answer the call. It's what I've done since Liam died—take care of his girlfriend.

I squeeze my eyes closed until voicemail picks up. When I open them and see the hoses sticking into Kate's nostrils, something inside me shatters. I can't keep doing this—needing Kate but unwilling to break it off with Ellie. I don't know if I can stop, though. Not after all this time.

Not after what I promised Liam.

"Why me, Kate? I'm a broken mess." I sigh, gliding my fingers over the exposed skin on her chest.

I can't figure out her hold on me. I just know that when I'm with her, it feels like she's beginning to piece me back together.

Today, Marcy has her laptop out, her eyes moving from one side to the other as she reads. Her concentration reminds me of the zones Liam used to get into when he studied. If I had to guess, this has always been her custom when Kate's in the hospital. Research the shit out of what's happening to her daughter. Find answers. Something to explain why Kate is suffering and how to fix it.

I understand Marcy. I crave answers too.

Unlike Marcy, though, I don't think there are any. Answers imply that life makes sense. That life's fair. But it's not, and no amount of research or hoping will change that. Life is just fucked up sometimes.

After lunch, Ellie texts me again. I stare at the screen, debating. Obviously, she needs me, but I know if I check the message, I'll end up high-tailing my ass out of here to give her what she wants—an escape.

My gaze settles on Kate. There's been no change since they admitted her, and I can't decide if that's good or not. No one seems bothered by it, so I guess I shouldn't be either. Maybe it's what's expected at this point. Still, what if she takes a turn for the worse and I'm not here?

Not just *not here*. Not here because I'm out fucking Ellie, drowning myself in her so that I don't have to deal with my own weaknesses.

No matter how much I want to be there for Ellie—numbing the both of us—I shouldn't.

With my eyes on Kate, I slide my finger across the screen to silence the phone. If I can't hear Ellie call me, I won't think about her.

I slip the phone into my pocket, hoping the decision doesn't come back to bite me in the ass. I've never *not* answered Ellie's calls.

Marcy has returned to her computer, so I pull a notebook out of my bag. I'd rather work on this song with my guitar in hand, but I don't want to disturb Marcy, and I sure as hell don't want any of the nosy nurses on this floor sticking their heads in here uninvited. They do that enough as it is.

As I brush my fingers over Kate's hand, I read what I wrote the other night. The song is damn promising, and the thought of singing it to Kate makes me smile. *Really* smile:

> *The right words never seem to come to mind*
> *So tell me you love me*

Or tell me you hate me
Tell me the world's not over me
No, the world's not over me.

I'm still scribbling over lyrics, tweaking them, when Mr. Browdy arrives after work. Marcy lays her laptop on the floor to greet him.

"Dr. Lowell said he's going to keep her under until her blood work improves," Marcy tells him.

"Any idea how long that might be?"

Marcy shakes her head in reply, and I glance away.

Did my dad know anything? *Isn't it his fucking job to know?*

Mr. Browdy clears his throat before he walks over to Kate's bed. Instead of addressing Kate, though, he says my name.

"Damian?"

I look up. "Yeah?"

He sets a sack on the nightstand and pulls out Styrofoam boxes. "I, uh, didn't know what you liked to eat, so I ordered you a burger and fries. Is that okay?"

The man brought me dinner?

"You didn't have to do that," I say.

"Kate mentioned once that you and she share a dislike for hospital food. It's my pleasure." He grins, handing me the box.

"Thank you."

"You're welcome."

Kate's parents sit opposite me, Kate's between us, and I wonder if this is the routine families follow in the hospital. Using the bed as a table with the patient as the centerpiece. I'm not sure if that's sort of funny or a tad bit creepy. Either way, I go with it.

"What are you working on?" Mr. Browdy asks, nodding at my notebook.

I'm not sure what he'd think of my music writing hobby. Normally, I don't give a flying fuck what adults think of me. They don't know me and they don't care to, so it's strange that I hesitate before I answer.

"It's a song I'm writing," I say.

"I noticed your guitar over there in the corner. You been doing that long?"

He seems genuinely interested. Huh.

"Yeah, since junior high." I don't mention that my father thinks it's a waste of time or that my mother was the one who encouraged and supported me.

Mr. Browdy grins. "I used to play some when I was your age. I never had any formal training, though."

Didn't see that coming. Cool.

"I stopped taking lessons a couple of years ago," I say.

After Mom died.

"You can learn a lot if you've got a good ear. Keep practicing. Music is a lifelong skill and well worth the effort you put into it," he says, and just like that, I feel more at ease.

"Yes, sir."

~*~

I can't sleep. Marcy conked out two hours ago, but I'm awake as Tammy comes in to check on Kate and take her vitals.

"How much longer do you think my dad will keep her like this?" I ask.

"Well," Tammy sighs, "he's keeping a close eye on her blood work and—"

"That's not what I asked," I interrupt.

Tammy scribbles on Kate's chart before her eyes land on me. "Kate's cancer came back more aggressive this time. There's no telling how long her body will take to fight the virus off, but I promise, Damian, your dad is doing everything he can."

From where I'm sitting, it doesn't look like Dad is doing shit. The longer I'm in this room with Kate and she's not responding, the more pissed off I get. Has he even been here to check on her today?

My next question is on the tip of my tongue, but I have to force myself to ask it. "Is she going to be okay? No bullshit, Tammy."

Tammy's gaze moves to Kate's face. She sees what I do: a girl that doesn't deserve to be here. A girl on the edge of her life.

"Honestly, Damian, I don't know."

With the uncertainty Tammy laid out, the need to protect myself kicks in. I have to separate myself from this. From Kate.

After Tammy leaves, I dig my phone out from my back pocket. As soon as the screen lights up, I already hate myself for what I'm about to do. Maybe I can't be better, because when things begin to fuck up, I run to Ellie as often as she runs to me.

She's an addiction, like whiskey. It burns and soothes at the same time. I loathe it, I hate it, and I crave it.

I frown when I see how many missed calls and waiting text messages I have, all from Ellie. Nine texts and six calls since last night. She's never been this desperate before.

What the hell is wrong?

It's the only conclusion I come to, and it frightens the shit of me. If anything happened to Ellie and I wasn't there, I don't know what I'd do. I swore to Liam I'd take care of her, and I can't break that promise.

Those were the last words I ever spoke to my brother, and I won't let him down.

I take a final glance over my shoulder on my way out of Kate's room. "Goodbye, Katie," I mutter and close the door gently behind me.

Day 4

Ellie's texts are bothersome enough, and I only read two before I check my voicemail. Her sobs assault my ear so I can barely understand her. The second voicemail is slightly clearer, left thirty minutes after the first.

"Damian, please. I don't know who else to call. I need you. We're in the emergency room at your dad's hospital right now, and they haven't told us anything. Just…when you get this, please call me. I don't know what to do."

Emergency room? Shit!

I doubt she's still there since she left the voicemail last night. I scroll through the rest of her texts, skimming over them until I find a room number. Then, I take off toward the elevators. I have no idea where I'm going, so I'm glad I run into Tammy.

"Hey, Tammy," I say, stopping her. "Where's Internal Medicine?"

Her brows furrow in confusion. "Uh…it's clear on the other side of the hospital, on the first floor," she tells me, pointing east. "Keep moving in that direction and you'll run into it."

"Great, thanks," I say, offering no explanation.

While I'm riding down to the first floor, it dawns on me that I should have asked why someone would be admitted to Internal Medicine. I have no clue what to expect, or even if it's Ellie that's hurt. I sure as hell hope not.

Fuck! What was I thinking not answering her?

I jog down the hallways, keeping an eye out for the signs leading me to the right place. When I reach the nurses' station in the east corridor, I duck around the corner. I'm not in the mood for explaining myself to any of them. If I'd been smart, I would have grabbed a set of scrubs from storage closet on the oncology floor.

Room 111 has its door cracked open, but that's not what catches my attention. Like me, it seems Ellie can't sleep tonight either. She's sitting on the floor outside the room, legs curled up to her chest, eyes swollen from crying. Though, now it seems her tears have run dry. Her phone grasped in one hand, she stares at it before her fingers begin to move over the screen.

When she finishes, my phone goes off. This time, I check it immediately:

Where are you, Damian?

I don't hesitate. Seeing her like this is messing me up.

Right here. Look up.

As soon as I send the text, her phone rings, and I'm taken aback by her ringtone for me. The chorus to Cassadee Pope's "I Wish I Could Break Your Heart" sounds from her phone. I don't get the connection.

Even from where I stand, I see the glisten of moisture gathering in Ellie's eyes as she reads my text. Her lips part when she lifts her head, her gaze meeting mine from across the hall. Even without makeup, she's beautiful. I'm so relieved she's not the one admitted that I let out a sigh of relief.

She drops her phone on the floor beside her and readies herself to stand up. I shake my head and walk over, sliding down the wall to sit beside her.

"Ellie—" I start.

She sniffles and rotates into me, wrapping her arms around my neck and pushing herself hard against me. Tears drop onto me as she buries her face into my shoulder.

"Baby, you've got to tell me what's wrong." I pull her to me, nervous. I haven't seen her like this since Liam died, and back then, we were both a mess.

"Just…hold me, okay?" she rasps out.

I nod against her, wishing I could comb my fingers through her hair, but she has it piled on top of her head. Instead, I massage my fingertips over the back of her neck to soothe her. Damn, I wish I would've answered my phone last night, I think again. She needed me—and not for sex.

Nurses I don't recognize pass us, and I'm glad as hell they don't know me. Lately, I've found myself caring about what the oncology nurses think of me, like if they approve, maybe there's hope that I can be good enough for Kate.

And god damn it all, I've fucked that up again, being down here with Ellie. Already my body is reacting to having her against me. Her scent, so different from Kate's, flows through me, and I have to reach between us to adjust my boner.

When Ellie leans back and wipes her eyes, I miss her in my arms. Having her close to me felt like I was doing something for her. Now, I'm just the douche bag sitting beside her.

"I'm sorry," she apologizes, though I don't know for what.

"What happened, Elle?"

She swipes her palms down her thighs, and I can't help staring at the motion and wishing her jeans were on the floor. Because damn, those thighs around me are something else.

I'm rock hard at the thought.

"Um, yesterday when Dad came home from work, Mom said she thought he looked pale. I went over for dinner, and he was acting strange. Then he collapsed. I called 911. They said it was a massive stroke, and today they said it caused a lot of damage. That…that he won't be able to walk again." Her fist flies to her mouth to hold back the sobs.

At almost twenty, she shouldn't have to deal with this yet, but Ellie's parents are older. I don't know what to do for her except gather her up in my arms again. Her head rests on my shoulder, and I feel her lips press against my neck.

From Ellie, I don't need more of an invitation

than that. I've been there for her in lesser circumstances, and I know how to take her mind off things when shit hits the fan. It's what brought us together.

"Come on. I'll help you get to sleep," I say, extending my hand.

She hesitates, glancing at the door to her father's room. "I don't know if I should leave my mom by herself. What if…?"

Ellie reminds me of Liam—always considerate. It's probably why they were so good for each other. Like Liam, Ellie's one of the good ones—unlike me.

Instead of lingering in the past, I do what I do best: I take Ellie down Asshole Lane with me. "She's a big girl, Elle. She'll be fine for a while."

I don't wait for her to decline my offer. I take Ellie's hand and lead her outside. Sure, she should stay with her mom, just like I should be in Kate's room right now, but I justify my actions by convincing myself I'm taking care of Ellie. I'm keeping my promise to my brother.

Flurries swirl around us as we jog to my car. It's parked on the back edge of the parking lot, and at this time of night, there are few vehicles this far out. I dig out my keys from my pocket and unlock the doors.

"Backseat," I say, then I feel up her ass as she climbs in.

After I shut her in, I slide into the driver's seat to start the car and crank the heat. It's damn cold outside, and I need Ellie to be comfortable, not distracted.

I jump to the backseat with her and get to work, sucking on her neck. She moans softly and tilts her head to the side, giving me better access. Fuck, I missed this.

I move slow, even though I'd rather tear her clothes off and plunge inside her as quickly as possible. I need her on me, but I want her to enjoy it, so I take my time.

Her gaze drifts out the window, and I wonder if she's worried about someone catching us. I pull her back to me and keep her mouth busy on mine. No one is out here except us.

A vision of Kate lying in her hospital bed, struggling with each breath, creeps into my mind. I push it away.

I can't think about her right now. Can't think about what Tammy said about her maybe not surviving.

I'm not strong enough to lose anyone else.

I fight through Kate's image and focus on Ellie. My hands slip under her shirt, pressing against her ribs. Soft, familiar flesh greets me, and I want more of it.

"Maybe we should…" Ellie trails off.

"Enjoy ourselves," I finish for her, pushing her up against the door and opening her knees to push myself against her sweet spot. I rock into her over and over.

Ellie's breath comes faster, her lips parting in response. I glide my tongue over her throat as she leans her head back. God, I want to devour her and leave nothing but pieces of both of us scattered on the floor. We can make all the excuses we want, but we're both here for the same reason: to forget. To drown ourselves in each other and pretend our lives make sense.

Before Kate. Before Liam.

At the thought, my movements speed up. I'm tired of thinking. Tired of breathing. I tug Ellie's shirt over her head, not taking the time to enjoy the view of her breasts packed into her bra before I unhook it, freeing them into my palms.

I crush my lips onto hers as I roll both of her nipples between my thumbs and fingers. She loves when I do this, and I'm immediately rewarded with a breathless huff. She's squirming under me, and it's so fucking hot.

"Damian," Ellie whimpers in my ear, hardening me even more.

We know each other. After two years, I'm an expert at turning her on and vice versa. Together, we're safe.

Ellie gathers the back of my shirt into her hands and pulls it off me. She's not as eager as I am because she's too gentle, but I'm beyond caring. I'm losing myself in her body.

I trail my hands over her breasts, give them a good squeeze before I travel down her stomach and unbutton her jeans. I feel her tense a little, and I'm not sure why. It's not like her. But as long as she doesn't tell me to stop, we're good.

She doesn't, averting her gaze as I slip her jeans over her hips. I brush my fingers up her thighs and skim the edge of her underwear, waiting for a response. A shiver, a smile, a quiet moan. I get none of these things.

It's okay. Whatever is bothering her at the moment, I'm in the perfect position to relax her. And I need her relaxed so that I can let go of my worries too, especially since I haven't had a drink in a couple of days.

"Come here," I say, pulling her panties down. She raises her ass to help me, and I ignore the distant look in her eyes. It'll be gone in a few minutes, I'll make sure of it.

Now that she's naked, I shimmy out of my own jeans and sit in the middle of the backseat. I glide my hand up her inner thigh and separate her, massaging her so I know she's ready.

And damn is she ready.

A small moan escapes her at my touch, and she locks her beautiful blues on me. A flicker of pain flashes in them before she looks away. If I was a decent guy, like Liam was, I'd back down at this point. I know she's thinking she shouldn't be out here with me. She should be inside with her mother, watching over her father.

I know, because it's what I'm thinking too. With Kate.

Except I'm not a decent guy. I'm not Liam, and right now I'm in my car with his girlfriend.

I shrug it off because I'm so goddamn horny. It's been three days—too fucking long. I grab Ellie's hips and guide her to my lap.

"You're still taking that pill, right?" I ask unnecessarily.

Two years ago we made this deal. Ellie had been my first and my brother had been hers. If we're with anyone else, condoms are a must; however, with each other, we don't bother. I want to feel every inch of her; it's our way of prioritizing, I guess. I've had other girls when Ellie's been unavailable, but she only fucks me. I don't complain.

"Yeah. We're good," she answers, distant. She's staring out the back window toward the hospital.

I take her chin between my forefinger and thumb and bring her mouth to mine, distracting her from her guilt. Mine lingers, reminding me that I'll pay for this later.

It's not like I've made a commitment to Kate. I'm not in love with her.

That thought urges me on, and I position Ellie over me. Her knees sink into the seat on both sides of me as she dips down, my dick sliding into her.

Fuck yes.

She clenches her muscles, gripping around me as she slides up and relaxing when she glides back down. The feeling she creates on me almost makes me forget about Kate. Almost.

Ellie works on me like she knows what she's doing, even though I catch her gaze flick up to the hospital. When I see it, I cup a breast and draw it to my mouth. It's enough for her lips to form an O, and she closes her eyes, falling into the sensation.

If I can keep her like this, in a state of ecstasy, she'll be moaning soon. If not, our little escape from reality will suddenly become a lot of work for me. Distracted girls don't come easily.

I rock her hips into me, pressing deeper inside her. My fingers drift over her bare back, and I angle her head to the side so I can nibble on her neck. She usually loves when I do this, and tonight is no exception. She lets out a gasp, her breath wafting over me in ragged puffs of air.

I have her now.

I lean back against the seat, feeling every tiny motion of her body. Thoughts of Kate sneak into my head again, how this proves my father is right about me. That *I'm* right about me. I don't deserve that girl.

Ellie rides me faster, and my hands automatically grip onto her ass to help her out. I push into her, my own orgasm rising within me. Ellie throws her head back and cries out in pleasure, giving me the go ahead to release myself inside her. My heart races as I push as deep as I can.

Her arms slink around my neck, and she nestles into me, laying her head on my shoulder. It's more personal than what's typical for us, and it momentarily catches me off guard. As if realizing that, she pulls away.

"Uh, sorry," she mutters under her breath. Then she slides off me and begins to grab for her clothes on the floor. "I should head back in there, Damian, but thanks. Hopefully I'll be able to fall asleep now."

I nod. "Yeah, me too."

As she gathers her stuff, she hands me mine. Silently, we scramble to get dressed, and already guilt sinks into the pit of my stomach. I dread going back to the third floor. To Kate.

I'm a fucking asshole.

Not only to her, but to Ellie, too.

God, I need a drink. Instead, I snatch the pack of cigarettes in my glove box. I pull one out and shut the car door behind me.

Ellie begins to walk across the parking lot. When she notices I'm not with her, she turns around.

"You coming?"

I shake my head and light up. "Go ahead."

Ellie flashes me a disapproving glare. She's used it on me before, and I know what's coming. She takes a few steps toward me, frowning. "You need to quit that, Damian. It's not good for you."

I laugh. "Thanks for the advice, Elle."

"I mean it. Liam would be disappointed—"

"In this?" I cut her off, holding up the cigarette. "Yeah, well, I'm sure Liam would be disappointed in a lot of things if he were here. But he's not, Elle. He's gone."

She slinks up to me, and I can feel her body heat radiating off her and filling the small space between us. "Your brother loved you, Damian. He wanted what was best for you…and so do I."

I take another drag and blow the smoke in her face. She doesn't flinch at my asshole gesture. "That's charming, Ellie. Really."

"You're better than this," she says, nodding at the cigarette, but I doubt that's all she means by her statement. "Liam would have wanted—"

I'm done with her lecture. "I know what he would have wanted." I toss the butt and shove my hands into my pockets. "It's the same thing Dad wants. I'll never live up to it, though, Ellie, so stop. No matter what I do, it won't bring Liam back."

I hold her gaze for a second longer, until I see tears brimming in her eyes. Then, in true Damian style, I sweep past her and jog back into the hospital. As I pass the gift shop, I notice the sales lady is still there doing inventory. I duck inside and sweet talk her into letting me buy up all the flowers they have. It won't stop the guilt that's threatening to consume me, I know that.

I've royally fucked up again. With Kate. With Ellie. With my dead brother.

I take a detour and lay a bouquet of flowers at Ellie's dad's door. After how I left her outside, she'll know they're from me.

Then I take the stairs up to the third floor. With my arms loaded down with flowers, it's difficult to open the door quietly, but I manage. Marcy's still asleep in the extra bed; my arrival doesn't disturb her.

I set the flowers with vases on Kate's nightstands, and the rest I dump on the window ledge to deal with in the morning. Except one single red rose. I pull it out of the bundle and walk over to Kate's bed and my empty chair.

Slowly, I scoot the chair as close to Kate's head as I can. Beside me, the machines beep in a steady rhythm, and the sound works to undo me. I sit down, holding the rose in my hand, debating. Asking someone for their forgiveness is one thing, asking it of yourself is another.

I need to decide what the fuck I'm doing. Why, after everything that's happened, I always seem to wind up here. Beside *this* girl.

I don't know how much time passes as I watch her, fighting to come up with some logical reason for why she captivates me. The only thing I conclude is how pissed off I am at myself for letting her down tonight. It doesn't make a lick of sense. Neither she nor Ellie is my girlfriend, and I don't owe them anything.

Still, it eats away at me.

Finally, I lay the rose by Kate's ear and run my fingertips over her face. So beautiful. So fragile. So innocent.

So not me.

All of my faults, my weaknesses, my mistakes rush out in one short sentence. "I'm sorry, Katie."

When I finally wake up, it's after noon. Marcy is gone, leaving Kate and me alone. I should enjoy this. But knowing what I did last night, how I left her for another girl, being alone with her seems like a moment I'm not worthy of.

I slide my hand over her face, any part of bare skin I can find. Touching Kate isn't like touching Ellie. It's like touching something so precious, so special that each time your fingers glide over it, you savor every second. Because someday it might disappear, and you'll never get a second chance to appreciate it.

That's what I'm doing now. Appreciating her.

I can't lose this girl.

Kate, with all her strength, all of her goodness, is exceptional. All that Kate is, I want to hold in my arms and keep for myself. I want her to belong to me and only me.

Broken, undeserving me.

I shake my head. How many times have I had to

apologize to her? Too many, and I know there'll be more. It's what scared shitless people do. Make mistakes and hide behind them.

My mind travels back to last night with Ellie, how I treated her. Liam would never have done that. My brother was a goddamn saint that I'll never live up to.

I clench the muscles in my jaw, my fingers trailing down Kate's neck. Her skin is too cool. The soft, smooth flesh warms under my touch, and I'd give anything to warm her entire body this way.

Kate needs her own Liam. Someone I'll never be, but for her, I'm going to try my damnedest. I promised her that, and I'm doing a shitty job at keeping my end of our bargain.

"That all changes right now, baby," I finish out loud, hoping she can hear me. "This time is for real. From here on out, you won't even recognize me.

Two hours later when Leslie walks in, I smile at her. Marcy peeks up from behind her laptop and nods a hello.

"Here," I say, standing up. "You can sit here if you want."

I don't want to give up my seat, especially to the nurse who hates my guts, but it's what Liam would have done. You know, think of others before yourself and all that shit.

Leslie's lips move like she's going to answer me, but no sound comes out. I've made her speechless, which is quite an accomplishment, really. I laugh to myself. Had I known this trick earlier, I would've used it more often.

"Um, thank you, Damian, but I can't stay long," she finally says. "Any change?" she asks Marcy.

"No. Her blood work shows no improvement. I don't know what else can be done for her," Kate's mom says. Her mouth tightens into a line.

Leslie hugs her, offering words of encouragement I can barely hear. Liam-like, I pull two tissues from the box beside me and hand them to Marcy when Leslie lets go of her.

Marcy dabs her cheeks. "Thank you, Damian."

"You're welcome. Can I get you anything else? A cup of coffee?"

"That's very kind of you. Yes, coffee sounds great."

Honestly, I should have been doing these things for Marcy all along. She's not taken aback by my sudden offer, though. Like me, she's been absorbed in her own world the last few days.

Leslie's expression, however, has me chuckling. Her wide-eyed gaze follows me out of the room, digging into my back. This isn't the me she's grown to loathe.

That Damian has been an asshole to the nursing staff, Leslie especially. Besides my father, Leslie is my go-to person when it comes to what I'm supposed to do around here. I don't listen to her, though, and the old Damian didn't give a damn about her working extra hours to make up for what I failed to do.

As I make my way back to Kate's room from the cafeteria, I pass Leslie in the hallway.

"Damian?" she says, stopping me.

"Yeah?"

I smile at her again, enjoying how my abrupt change in demeanor is freaking her out.

"Um…" She blinks. Then twists and points in the direction of Kate's room, not saying anything comprehensible. "Uh…"

Damn, she's flustered. It's freaking hilarious.

"Leslie," I say, "I know that since Kate's been here, I haven't been working, which adds to your load, and I'm sorry about that. If you need me for anything, you know where to find me."

Leslie's jaw drops open for a nanosecond before she snaps it closed. I may have overdone that offer. Too much too soon.

I don't wait for a reply, but continue down the hall.

See? I can be a decent human being. Like Kate.

Like Liam.

That evening, I order in pizza for the Browdys, the nursing staff, and myself. The confused expressions on some of the nurses' faces were golden. This was not the same person who smashed a hospital window last month and showed up drunk on a weekly basis.

I even gathered up all the empty carry-out boxes and took them to the janitor's closet. Talk about going the extra mile.

Now, it's midnight and Marcy is asleep on the other bed. I've had my phone on silent all day, in case Ellie tried to call. How can I be a saint and tend to Liam's girlfriend at the same time? I haven't figured that part out yet, but the last thing I want to do is have to apologize to Kate again.

I stuff the phone in my back pocket without looking at it. Then, two minutes later, I dig it back out and check the messages. There's only one. From Ellie:

Me too.

This is her response to my floral apology, but for the life of me, I can't figure out why she's sorry. I'm the one who took advantage of her, yelled at her, and left her alone in the parking lot.

I don't dwell on it, though. I'm too tired. Being the good ol' boy is exhausting. How could Liam stand it? I slide the phone back into my pocket and rest my head over my arms on top of Kate's bed. I'm asleep in no time.

Day 5

I grimace at the sunlight that pours into the room, waking me up. When Liam was alive, he'd get up at the butt crack of dawn and either run or swim before anyone else was up. Sometimes, he'd even have breakfast made for everyone. Maybe the new Liam-Damian hybrid I'm working on can leave that part out. I'm not a morning person.

"Good morning." Marcy's voice greets me, and I squint at her. She's already showered, dressed, and back on her laptop, nursing a cup of coffee.

"Right," I answer, rubbing a palm down my face. I need to wake up, get ready, and do a repeat of yesterday. No mistakes today.

I grab my bag and head to the private bathroom. For a hospital, the water pressure in the shower is pretty decent. When I'm shaved and dressed, I wear a content expression that doesn't belong to me and walk out, ready to fetch some breakfast for Marcy and me.

"I'm thinking biscuits and gravy today," I say, dropping my bag in the far corner of the room.

"What can I bring up for you, Marcy?"

She takes a sip of coffee and peers at me from over the rim. It takes a few seconds before she speaks. When she does, her motherly tone shines through.

"Damian, that's very sweet, but I already ate. Why don't you go ahead?"

Hesitant, my gaze skims over Kate. Even though her mom will be with her, I hate to leave. My record shows that I screw up when I leave this room, and I'm trying so damn hard to be deserving of her. Hell, I barely recognized myself yesterday.

But, as much as I dislike hospital food, I'm starving, and really, their biscuits aren't too bad.

"Okay. I'll be right back," I say, mostly to Kate.

On the first floor, I round the corner into the cafeteria. I load my plate, grab an apple for later, and swipe my hospital ID card with the cashier. As I go to take my food upstairs, I see Ellie out of the corner of my eye. She's sitting by herself in the far corner of the cafeteria, her gaze trained outside. I should stay on my trajectory as planned, but then Ellie bows her head, covering her face with her palms. Instantly, I divert and walk toward her instead.

I stay focused on her as I cross the room. She doesn't move. Except when I get closer, I see her shoulders trembling. Her hands muffle the soft sobs.

"Ellie?" I say quietly so I don't startle her.

She sniffles and dabs a napkin over her cheeks. I slide my tray onto the table and pull out a chair opposite her. She doesn't acknowledge me, keeping her head down.

"What's going on?" I ask when she doesn't speak.

Ellie purses her lips and stares at her untouched food. I don't know why she doesn't want to look at me, so I scoot into the chair right beside to her and reach my hand up to her face, turning her head to me.

"What happened, Elle?" I ask again.

Whenever something goes wrong, Ellie tries to get a hold of me, but the last text I received from her was two nights ago.

Her eyes close, and a tear slips from one of them. I hold her chin between my thumb and forefinger, so when she opens her eyes, she'll see me. See that I'm here for her.

Ellie's lips tremble as she works to contain her sobs. Eventually, though, her eyelids lift, and I'm staring into the blue irises that I've grown to know so well. They glisten with moisture.

This moment, right here, takes me back to the nights when she broke down in my bedroom after Liam died. Ellie is hurting, and the fact that she won't talk to me about it frustrates me. For the last two years, she's come to me with everything, even stupid girly shit that I don't give a rat's ass about.

And for two years, I've been there for her.

"Come on, Ellie, talk to me," I encourage her, my voice low and void of the irritation I feel over her silence.

It takes her a few seconds, and I can see in her expression that she's debating whether to tell me or not. Finally, she sighs.

"My dad…he, uh…" She licks her lips, holding

the bottom one between her teeth. "The stroke did a lot of damage to his brain. He can't walk. He can barely talk, and Damian…"

Tears fall down her cheeks, and I let go of her chin to wipe them away.

"He doesn't remember me," she breathes out. She pauses, holding her breath. As she exhales, she reaches for me. Her face burrows into my neck making her next words barely audible. "I can't do this again, Damian. I can't lose anyone else."

I get it. God, I get it.

Ellie and I understand pain, how it eats at you until there's no other option than to numb it before it consumes you. They say that whatever doesn't kill you makes you stronger, but for us, it's only taught us that we can't handle this. Both of us are weak. Too weak to survive another round of heart-wrenching pain.

I hold her close and kiss her head. Like Ellie's dad, Kate's still alive, yet every second that passes and she doesn't wake up, I feel her slipping away. I don't know if she hears me, and if she does, does she equate my voice with me? Am I in her dreams like she's in mine?

I don't know what to say to comfort Ellie. Liam would know, but I'm not good at this stuff. Instead, I tighten my arms around her to protect her because I can't fix this. Not the way I used to.

I lean my head against hers, allowing my mind to wander to Kate and me. I'm with Ellie instead of her again. And I'm justifying it by telling myself it's because I'm keeping my promise to my brother, but I'm beginning to think I might be lying to myself. In all honesty, Ellie is comfortable. Safe.

Kate isn't.

Kate is a stick of dynamite, and leukemia is holding the detonator.

But I've made up my mind; I'm going to be there for Kate. All the way. Until she tells me otherwise.

Ellie unwraps her arms from around my neck and leans back in her chair. "I'm sorry, Damian. I just have a lot on my mind right now," she says, drying her face with her sleeve.

I shake my head. "No, it's fine, Elle." My next words spill out before I can stop them. "Whenever you need me, I'll be here for you."

Her eyes cut to me, and she holds my gaze. She knows me well, knows I've been distracted lately. She's not sure whether to believe my offer, and quite frankly, neither am I.

Slowly, she nods. "Your breakfast is cold," she says, changing the subject.

"It's okay. I'm not hungry anyway." My appetite has faded completely. I slide the tray across the table and pick it up. "Are you sure you'll be all right?"

"Yeah, go," she says, folding both hands around her Styrofoam coffee cup. "You probably have a lot to do today."

I stand up. The obligation I feel to stay here with her tugs at me, but my need to be upstairs with Kate overpowers it. Even so, I glide my fingers down the side of Ellie's face. "Call me anytime, Elle."

My not staying speaks volumes, and Ellie realizes it, too. Two years of being there for her every beck and call is coming to an end. She doesn't answer me right away, her eyes not wavering from the window.

"Sure," she says, and by her tone I'm not sure she will.

I go to leave, take a couple of steps, then turn back around. "Ellie?"

She doesn't answer.

I continue anyway, because I need to know. "What was it about Liam that made you fall for him?"

At the mention of his name, she lifts her head. I don't talk about Liam. Not the way Ellie does. Her shoulders rise and fall, and for a moment, I wonder if she's going to ignore me. But a second later, she swivels in her chair.

She tucks the locks of loose hair behind her ears before her eyes flick up to me. She doesn't answer right away, but when she does, her voice is soft. "Liam was genuine. What you saw was what you got."

I stay with Kate for the rest of the day. Marcy's here too, working away on her laptop, searching for a miracle that can save her daughter. I hope she finds one.

At some point, I pick up my guitar and work through the song I haven't finished. I'm mumbling the lyrics I have so far when what Ellie said about Liam enters my mind. Then suddenly, memories of the dinner Kate and I shared before she got sick takes its place. That night, I'd lost it in front of her, needing her like I've never needed anyone.

I can't make sense if it on my own, so I allow my thoughts to spill out onto the page:

> *There are no reasons*
> *That you're searching for*
> *I haven't left the door open long*
> *Please don't stop looking*
> *I need your understanding*
> *I need you to make sure I land on my feet*
> *Tell me you love me*
> *Tell me you want me*
> *Tell me that the world's not over me*

The one-sided deal I made with Kate seeps into my memory: if she'd wake up, I'd be better. Like Liam.

The rest of the song flows out of me:

> *The world's not over me*
> *Come find me*
> *In my hiding place*
> *I swear I'll pray for you*
> *I don't know if you'll follow through,*
> *but if you do*
> *I'll be waiting for you*
> *To tell me you love me*
> *That you hate that the world*
> *Isn't over me*
> *The world isn't over me*

Strumming the last chord, I let it reverberate. I swallow, stunned at the realizations that came as I sang. I scan over the words again. It's not perfect, but it will be.

Sometimes, the secrets of your life are revealed at the most inopportune times, and in the places you least expect.

Kate's black diary on the nightstand catches my eye, and it's like a light clicks on in my head. After all the shit I've done that she knows about—that I've done *to* her—she's with me. Five days ago, she was with me.

Me. Not Liam.

Me.

I set my notebook aside and stand up. All I see is Kate. Even lying there, the girl takes my breath away. Seven years of fighting this disease, and, essentially, she's done it alone. But not anymore.

Careful of the cords and tubes snaking into her, I climb onto the all-too-small hospital bed. I need to have her close. Yesterday, I'd been so busy trying to please everyone, I'd spent less than ten real minutes with the only person I care about pleasing.

I reach across her, sliding my fingers down her face. Her skin is warmer than it has been, and I can't help thinking that's a good sign. The coolness bothered me. Like she was dying.

"Katie," I whisper into her ear. "Come back to me, baby."

I brush my lips over her cheek, savoring how my breath wafts over her before it reverts back to me, now carrying her sweet scent.

I squeeze my eyes closed and gently press my forehead against hers. I'm close to losing it again. I shouldn't need Kate this much. I shouldn't need

anyone this much.
     But I do.

Day 6

I wake up before the sun rises. My hand sweats, and it takes me a second to realize why. I've had Kate's hand clasped in mine all night. I let go, worried that I've overheated her. Wiping my palm on my jeans, I stand up to check the monitor that keeps track of her vitals. I'm not sure what I'm seeing, but no alarms are going off. Regardless, I lay the back of my hand over Kate's forehead.

She's warm. Much warmer than earlier.

Again, I peer up at the screen. Damn it. I wish I knew what the hell those numbers meant.

My gut tells me something's not right. I'm beginning to panic because I have no idea what's wrong, and I can't do shit about it. I can't stop what's happening.

For a second, I consider rousing Marcy. I shoot a quick glance over my shoulder. Marcy seems to be sleeping peacefully for once, and she's in the same helpless boat as I'm in. No, I won't disturb her.

Instead, I lean over Kate and kiss her head. "I'm going to find Tammy, baby. I'll be right back."

I swallow hard because I don't want to leave her. I could push the call button, but I don't want to worry Marcy. She has enough to deal with, and if I'm wrong, then I've woken her up for no reason.

God, I hope I'm wrong.

My gaze trails over Kate one last time before I exit the room, leaving the door cracked behind me. There's one nurse—Pat—at the nurses' station, and she's a newbie on this floor. I doubt she knows anything about Kate's case.

"Where's Tammy?" I demand. Fuck the niceties.

Her brows furrow at me. My tone catches her off guard. "Um, she's making her rounds. Can I help you, Damian?" she asks, scowling—yeah, *scowling*—at me.

Perfect. She knows my name, and judging by her expression, my reputation has preceded me. I'm not going to get anywhere with this nurse.

I slap the counter. "No, you can't. What room is she in?" I'm not the guy I was yesterday. Hell, I'm not *that* guy at all.

The nurse shakes her head. "I'm not at liberty to give you that infor—"

"I don't give a fuck what information you're not at liberty to give," I say, my tone dropping low. I don't handle these situations well, especially when it involves someone I care about. And this nurse is *really* starting to piss me off.

"Hospital policy states—"

Is she serious?

"Something is wrong with Kate Browdy, and Tammy knows her case. Where is she?"

Pat checks her computer then shakes her head.

"Kate Browdy is fine. If something were wrong, I'd know about it. Now, visiting hours don't begin until—"

I've had enough of this bullshit. And right now, I'm desperate.

"I need to speak with Tammy, and I need to speak with her now. So, if you don't give me what I need, I will stalk up and down this hallway, slamming every goddamn door open until I find her. Do you understand me?"

Even as I say it, I know it's an empty threat. I might be an asshole, but this is the pediatric oncology floor, and there are young children in those rooms. However, I'm counting on my reputation to make this work.

I see a hint of fear in her eyes, and I'm sure she's close to giving in.

She doesn't.

"I'm calling security," she says, reaching for the phone.

Shit!

I grab her wrist before she touches the receiver. She fixes her stare on me, eyes wide.

"Tammy," I repeat.

Kate's on the verge of something bad, and I'm close to losing it with Pat.

The nurse's nostrils flare, and I think she's shaking a little. I don't let go, though. In fact, I squeeze her wrist a little tighter for emphasis. I'm not thinking of the repercussions for my actions. I'm a man on a mission.

Her breath hitches at my grip, and I cock my head to the side. "I'm fucking serious," I grind out.

Her eyes flick up and focus behind me. I spin around to see Tammy exiting a patient's room halfway down the corridor.

I toss the nurse's hand away and jog down the hallway. She'll probably have security on the phone in one second flat, but I've got more pressing matters on my mind. I've dealt with hospital security before. They know me well.

"Tammy," I say when I catch up to her.

She must see the panic on my face because her brows knit together in concern. "What's wrong, Damian?" she asks.

"Kate. She's warm, and—"

I'm cut off by alarms ringing at the nurses' station. My head snaps toward the sound, and I know it's Kate even before Pat darts the short distance into her room.

"Fuck!"

I run down the hall, Tammy on my heels. I swing into Kate's room. Roused from her sleep, Marcy's on her feet at the foot of Kate's bed, and Nurse Bitch is just studying the goddamn printout!

Tunnel-visioned, I sweep behind Marcy. With the lights on, I see how pale Kate is. How her lips are no longer pink. It's a complete one-eighty from the flushed face I left her with. Like all of the blood has drained from her.

Pat yelps when I shove her out of my way. "Kate, I'm here. I'm here, Kate." I fold her hand into mine.

"You need to step back, young man," I hear her say. I ignore her because if she'd have only listened to me in the first place, then…

Her voice rises when she says my name. "Damian, you need to—"

"Pat," Tammy cuts her off, shaking her head. Tammy's all business, and I could fucking hug her for it. "Page Doctor Lowell."

Pat shuts up, nods once, and hurries out of the room.

"Is it that bad?" Marcy asks, her arms wrapped around herself.

Tammy checks Kate's IV before answering. "Her blood pressure's dropped, and it's straining her heart." She sighs, her eyes teetering to me. "I'm sorry, but when Dr. Lowell arrives, you'll need to wait outside."

I open my mouth to object when Marcy says, "Of course. Whatever you need." She's on the verge of tears.

I rake my hand through my hair, frustrated. The last thing I want is to leave Kate here alone. But I feel myself nodding my agreement.

Slowly, I raise Kate's fingers to my lips. "You're in good hands, baby."

I don't care that Tammy heard me and is now staring at me. I let Kate's hand slip from mine, and it takes everything I have to follow Marcy out.

As soon as we leave, I see my dad rushing toward us. He doesn't look at me, not that I expect him to. Like me, his only concern is Kate.

I watch him enter Kate's room, Pat right behind him. At the same time, I see Matt the security guard step off the elevator. Perfect fucking timing.

"I'll go grab us some coffee," I tell Marcy.

"Thank you, Damian," she says, and walks down

the hallway to the Commons.

I, on the other hand, saunter toward Matt. The man doesn't look happy.

"I received a call from Patricia that you assaulted her. Damian—"

Assaulted? What the fuck?

I hold up a palm. "Now's not a good time, man."

Matt gives me a skeptical onceover and sniffs the air around me. "Have you been drinking?"

I wish.

"No. Kate needed help. It was an emergency. The shit with Pat, dude that was all a misunderstanding." He doesn't know who Kate is, and I doubt he cares.

Matt glares at me, and I don't think he's buying my story. I need to do something because I'm not getting kicked out of here. Not today.

"Where's Patricia?" he asks.

"I told you. There was an emergency. She's in there." I point toward Kate's closed door.

"Damian," he starts, "you have a history here, and assault is a very serious accusation."

"I'm not leaving. Not as long as Kate's here in this hospital."

Matt sighs as he considers his next move. I'm resilient, and he knows it. No one on earth could get away with the shit I've evaded here. My dad's the best oncologist they have, and they don't want to lose him. It's the only reason I'm allowed inside.

"Tammy," he says, pushing past me.

I swing around to see her exiting Kate's room, her face solemn. What does it mean that she left? Her eyes bounce up to me for a split second before they fall on Matt.

I move in closer to hear them.

"—assaulted her," Matt finishes.

Again, Tammy's gaze flashes to me then back to the security guard. "It was a misunderstanding, Matt. We've all had a rough morning. I'll talk to Pat. Thank you for your quick response in this matter, but I assure you, everything is fine."

Mat hesitates. "Okay, then," he says, before he turns to me. "Stay out of trouble, Damian."

"Yes, sir," I mutter as he stalks away. "Tammy—"

"You really care about Kate, don't you?" she interrupts me.

All I can do is nod because I don't think I'm strong enough to say it out loud. "Is she okay?"

"They're still working on her. She's a tough girl."

"Yeah, she is."

"Hang in there, Damian," Tammy says, placing a hand on my shoulder. "Kate has a lot worth fighting for."

Kate's dad is with Marcy when I return to the Commons with our coffees. The Browdys sit at a small table, heads leaned in together.

"Thank you," Marcy says as I hand her the Styrofoam cup.

Wordlessly, I slump onto the sofa on the other side of the room by myself. I want to be alone with my thoughts. It's definitely not what Liam would do, but I'm done caring what he would do. Kate never wanted Liam. She didn't even know him, so I can begin fresh. I don't have his perfect-ass standard to live up to with her.

I drag a hand down my face, sliding my fingers over the stubble on my jaw. Six days ago, I was considering leaving Kate because *I* couldn't handle her disease. Because *I* wasn't strong enough.

Today, I'm still not strong enough, but thanks to Ellie, I realize that I don't have to be. She didn't love Liam because he was perfect. No, she loved him because he was genuine.

Kate doesn't need me to be strong. She needs me to be there. To be *me*. The rest we can work out together.

Now all Kate has to do is beat the virus and wake the hell the up.

An hour passes, and beams of sunlight scatter through the blinds. No one has come in to give us an update on Kate's condition. My coffee is long gone, and I cross my arms.

I'm cold. I'm hot. I'm scared.

I'm so fucking scared.

Finally, my dad appears in the doorway. His face is long, tired. He glances in my direction before he approaches Kate's parents. I don't follow him over. I just sit here, watching as he speaks quietly to the Browdys.

Marcy's hand covers her mouth, tears slipping onto her cheeks. Mr. Browdy cradles her in his arms, and my heart drops into my stomach. Kate has to be okay.

The need to see her for myself overwhelms me.

Quietly, I slip out of the Commons and head to Kate's room. There's one nurse at the nurses' station, but she doesn't look up when I walk past. The door to Kate's room is shut, and I hesitate as I reach for the handle. I don't know what I'll find behind it, but I don't want to dwell on the possibilities, either.

I push the fear away and open the door.

The soft hum of machines greets me, and for once, it's a welcoming sound. But it's not enough to back me off the edge. That won't happen until I know she'll be okay. Hell, until she says my name.

Whoever left the room last closed the curtain. I gather the material in my hand and slide it back. She's lying there, hooked up like when I left her. I can't see if she's breathing. My eyes flick up to the monitor, and the first thing I notice is the steady heartbeat.

I hear myself exhale as relief floods through me like a damn breaking free.

She's alive.

My gaze returns to her. The same body I woke up to this morning rests on top of the mattress, but it's different. Stronger. More resilient.

This girl. This beautiful girl in front of me amazes me with everything she is.

Her skin's not as pale as earlier. Her lips are pink again. I lean over her, my hands on either side of her head, smashing into her pillow. Closing my eyes, I hold my position over her, not touching her. I want to feel her warmth on my face, her breath on my mouth.

"It's just us, Katie," I whisper. "Give me

something to let me know you can hear me."

Closing my eyes, I wait. I don't move or breathe. She offers nothing, and I open my eyes to take her in. I lower myself until my nose grazes hers. Then I repeat the words I told her a week ago in front of the fireplace. This time I understand what I'm saying.

This time it's for real.

"Don't leave me, Katie. Don't leave me."

~*~

Kate is under constant supervision. If my father wants a nurse watching over her, that must mean he's worried. Dad's even been in Kate's room more than his typical once every twenty-four hours. The rest of the time, he's in his office. What the fuck is up with that? Why isn't he doing something to fix her?

I'm sick of waiting for him. He's had enough time. I may not know much about medicine, but I'm pretty damn sure that jacking her up on all these drugs is a shock to her system. Doc of the Year has spoken with the Browdys numerous times, but now *I* want answers.

I round the corner to the hallway that leads to his office. The door is cracked open, so I have no doubt he's in there. The thought pisses me off even more. He's a fucking oncologist. His job is to heal his patients, not sit on his ass in his damn office.

I shove the door open without knocking. As predicted, he's behind his desk, staring at his computer screen. He glances up and wipes his brow like he's been expecting this confrontation. Placing both hands on his desk, I lean forward.

"What's wrong with Kate? Why haven't you woken her up?" I demand.

He's got the calm doctor thing going on, which only fuels the fire in me. He removes his glasses like he has all the time in the goddamn world.

"Damian, you know I can't—"

I pound my hands on the wood. "I'm not in the mood for your doctor-patient confidentiality bullshit. Kate's obviously not out of the woods if you have a fucking nurse stationed in her room."

"Son, the rules have already been bent for you. You've been told more than you should about her situation, and I haven't said anything about you staying in her room all night," he says.

"Gee, thank you, king of the universe."

"But," he continues, ignoring me, "I can't discuss this with you, no matter how much you care about her."

"This isn't about me."

His eyebrows perk up. "Isn't it?"

I don't hesitate. "No. It's about Kate. All the drugs she's on are destroying her body." I have no right to question my dad's medical expertise, but I'm confident in my stance. I have to know that Kate will be okay.

He nods, like he's actually considering what I said. "I know what I'm doing, son."

"So why the hell are you holed up in here?" I push.

"What do you want me to do, Damian? Stand over her bed? I've been here at the hospital twenty-four-seven since I admitted her. I'm keeping a close eye on her, despite what you think. She's been my patient for seven years, and I want nothing more than to see her walk out of this hospital cancer-free." He's losing his cool some. Good.

"Then what are you doing to make that happen?" My voice dips low. I came for answers, and god damn it, I'm going to get them!

"Everything I can," he says through gritted teeth. He's trying to keep his composure, but he's beginning to fray.

I shake my head, annoyed. "It's not good enough. It's been six days. *Six days* and she hasn't even batted an eyelash!"

Now I've really gotten to him. He shoots out of his chair. "You need to let me do my job and stop questioning me. What is Kate to you, anyway? Because I'll be damned if I allow you to use her like you use Ellie. Kate's sick, Damian."

I'm shaking now. How dare he insinuate that I'm using her? I pick up a paperweight and hurl it at a fake Monet painting behind me. The glass shatters, and I spin around to face my father again.

"Fuck you!" I spit out.

"I know Ellie's father was admitted a few days ago. I also know that you met up with her." He steps out from behind his desk. Close enough for me to throw a punch into his face.

His voice lowers, his eyes drilling into me. "Let me tell you something, son. You'd better figure things out, because when Kate wakes up, you have a choice to make. She merits every happiness, and if you can't give her that, you need to walk away."

When *she wakes up?*

I have no reply to the rest of what he said. I don't want him to know that he's right. I'll end up fucking this up somehow.

I take a step toward him, glaring at him. He doesn't budge. I'm still pissed, but I got the answer I came for. Kate *will* wake up.

When I speak, my tone mimics his. Low and menacing. He made his point, now I will make mine.

"You told me once that Kate was different. That her disease makes her different, and I want to tell you that you're wrong. Yeah, Kate's different, but it isn't leukemia that makes her that way. She doesn't let the cancer define her, and *that's* what makes her so damn special."

Day 7

Kate remained stable the rest of yesterday, and by the time Mr. Browdy left for the night, so had the nurse. Dad even made a couple extra appearances in Kate's room after our fallout.

I have a hard time sleeping, and from the sound of sheets rubbing together in the other bed, so does Marcy. Even though the Doc said Kate was in the clear for now, it does nothing to ease my mind.

At three a.m. I stop trying to sleep. I scoop up Kate's hand and hold it to my lips. The temperature of her skin has returned to normal, making slipping into bed with her difficult to resist. I don't, though, because I don't want to overheat her.

Quietly, I slide my chair up so that I'm closer to Kate's head. Even though I assume Marcy's awake, I speak softly to Kate anyway. I'm beyond caring who hears.

"We should go to Disney World," I say, recalling the list of activities she wants to do. "My parents took Liam and me a couple of times when we were younger." I snicker as a memory surfaces. "There's this, uh, kids' roller coaster that goes through a barn. It has Goofy and pals shape cut out as if they'd burst through the wall. I was six and Liam was nine, and he wanted to ride that thing so bad, but I took one look at it and freaked out. Mom said she'd go with me to the teacups again instead and Dad could ride with Liam on the evil roller coaster."

I smile to myself, thinking of what my brother did next. Even as a kid, he was fucking perfect. "But Liam said no. He didn't want to ride on anything if I couldn't go with him. Then he wrapped an arm around my shoulder and told me he'd never leave me behind." I pause as the image fades away. "We'll ride that one first, Kate, with our hands high up in the air like it's the scariest damn roller coaster there." I puff out a laugh at the thought.

I kiss Kate's hand and press it against my cheek. It's soft, smooth, and I'd give anything for her to curl her fingers around mine. I never knew holding someone's hand could be so intimate, so utterly incredible. But that's how it is with her.

If only she'd open her eyes.

Behind me, I hear Marcy shuffle around, and the bed creaks as she gets up. She rounds the end of Kate's bed and sits opposite me, taking Kate's other hand. Her lips purse, worry lines creeping from the corners of her eyes. For the longest time she doesn't say anything. She simply gazes at her daughter, like at any second Kate could slip away from us forever.

It's then I realize that Marcy's life has been made up of moments exactly like this one. Kate may be the one battling this disease, but the cancer has claimed other victims in its wake.

My father's words rip through me. He was right. Kate does deserve to be happy.

And yet…

"Sweetheart," Marcy murmurs, interrupting my thoughts, "you can wake up whenever you're ready. We're here for you, okay?"

I find myself staring at Marcy. At the tears glistening in her eyes. She's wearing the same expression I've seen on my father's face time and time again when he's concerned over a patient and thinks no one is paying attention. Desperation.

Marcy's eyes lift to meet mine, and she smiles at me. "It should be soon, Damian. Your father took her off the thiopental."

I swallow. "He did?"

She nods, hopeful. "Yes, earlier this afternoon, Tammy came in and switched her medication."

"This afternoon?" I repeat, thinking back.

"When you left to get coffee?"

That's what I had told her when I went to confront my dad. He'd given the order before I spoke to him.

Holy shit.

I never did fall asleep. Marcy got in a few hours, though. Right now, she's in the cafeteria eating lunch like I should be, but I can't leave Kate here after what her mother told me last night. Kate could wake up any minute, and I want to be here when she does.

I want to stare into those beautiful brown eyes of hers and let her captivate me.

I shift in my seat, and as I do, my phone digs into my ass. Leaning forward, I pull it out to check for messages. My brain has been so preoccupied with Kate over the last two days that Ellie's situation slipped my mind. I'd told her to call me, but I haven't heard my phone go off.

I should check up on her.

I tap my fingers on the phone. None of the choices I come up with sound like good options at the moment. I can't run down and see if she's here, not with Kate on the verge of waking up. Calling her in front of Kate seems like an asshole move, and I'm trying not to be an asshole. Besides, neither of these fall into the category of choosing Kate and letting Ellie go, which is what I need to do.

Yet somehow, *somehow*, I have to fulfill my promise to Liam.

I make the decision to shoot her a text:

Hey. You doing okay?

Short. Sweet. No bullshit.

I lay my phone on the bed and wait for an answer. It never takes Ellie long to return a text.

Twenty minutes later, when Marcy arrives with a sandwich for me, I'm still waiting. And I don't know what to think about it. Ellie's a big girl and can handle herself, but that's not what Liam would let her do. Especially not when she's hurting like she is.

Fuck. Me.

I glance at Kate, then at the monitor. I find myself doing that often. Yesterday, I asked the nurse what the numbers meant and what was considered normal, so now I have a frame of reference. They all look good.

"Marcy, I'm going to go speak with my dad for a minute. I'll be right back," I lie.

"We'll be here," she sings out. Even with so little sleep, Marcy is more chipper today. That's what hope does to people.

In the hallway, I head straight to the stairs instead of wasting time waiting for the elevators. I half jog to room 111, where Ellie's dad is supposed to be. The door is wide open, and a second later, a janitor backs out with a mop bucket.

"Hey," I say, stopping him. "Is Mark Vander Zee here?"

"Who?"

"The man who was admitted to this room? Where is he?"

"Uh, I don't know. I guess he left. I just cleaned the room."

"Yeah, thanks," I say as I turn away, digging my phone out of my pocket. Now that Kate's not beside me, I dial Ellie's number. After the fifth ring, her voicemail picks up.

"God damn it," I mutter.

I make my way back to the oncology floor, telling myself I've done all I can. If Ellie won't answer her phone, there's nothing I can do. Not even Liam could force her to do that when she sunk into stubborn mode. Sure, he'd go after her, but Ellie doesn't belong to me.

I choose Kate. It was never even a choice; it was me being a pussy because Ellie and I have a history. I know I'll have to tell Ellie eventually, but now doesn't seem like the best time. That and she's not answering her phone.

Standing outside of Kate's door, I smile to myself. Come hell or high water, I won't lose this girl.

Day 8

This morning, I wake up to a text from Ellie:

I'm fine, Damian.

That's it. And suddenly, I can breathe again. Not because she finally replied, but because last night, I didn't chase her.

No, last night, I did what I should have done a long time ago.

I let her go.

I'm not sure if that's the reason I see Kate differently right now, or if it's all the junk finally making its way out of her bloodstream that makes her seem brighter. She's not as pale; her skin even looks like it's taking on a healthy glow.

I'm counting down the hours. Ticking them off in my head. Tammy said the longer she's been under, the higher the risk of complications. She'd said more, but the word *complications* flashed red in my mind.

Forty-eight hours is the hoped-for time frame

according to Tammy, and we'd just passed hour twenty-one. Time couldn't move any slower.

"Anytime, Katie," I murmur against her hand that's been in mine since before the sun came up. I kiss it again, leaving my mouth on her.

In my downtime, I've worked some on the song, but mostly I've contemplated what to say to her when she wakes up. Again, I consider how my feelings for Kate mystify me. She's consumed my thoughts since day one. Both in good ways and bad. I'll never be able to live up to her. Yet she wants to be with me, and for the life of me, I can't figure out why.

Slowly, I graze my lips over the skin on the back of her hand. And that's when it happens. Her fingers constrict around mine for a second. Then she lets go.

I'm stunned for a moment before what happened sinks in. I bolt from my chair to stand over her. As I do, I tighten my grip on her hand.

I bend down, close to her ear, and whisper, "Do it again, Katie. Squeeze my hand."

I hold my breath, waiting. Waiting for the tiniest of movements.

A whole minute passes, and my lungs are on fire. I exhale and suck in air as if I'd completed a workout at the gym.

"Come on, Kate. Wake up," I say a little louder.

I stare at her, watching her chest rise and fall. But she offers no voluntary motion.

I glance at the clock and count down another hour. Twenty-two. The wait is fucking killing me.

Sitting back down, I push a hand through my

hair. I'm exhausted. Last night, I'd dozed off for a couple of hours, but it's been two days since I had a full night's sleep. I'm cool with it, though. I want to be awake when Kate opens her eyes.

I want to tell her…

My gaze slides over her again. Honest to God, she looks like she's only sleeping instead of working on coming out of an induced coma. I can't get over how much this girl infatuates me.

What the hell do I want to tell her?

That I'll be here for her.

Yeah, I guess. I can't promise anything else. Not right now, anyway. I need to get this Ellie thing under control first before I can even begin to figure out all that Kate means to me.

If I can ever be good enough for her.

~*~

My eyelids are dropping. Sleep is beckoning to me, and my body is rebelling against my mind. I can't sleep now. Not on hour twenty-six.

"Damian?" The sound of Marcy's voice jolts me to attention.

I rub my eyes as I face her. "Yeah."

"Sorry," she apologizes. She nods her head toward the door. "I'm going to go grab a coffee. Want some?"

"That would be great. Thank you."

She chuckles. "Okay, be right back."

As soon as she leaves, I pace the room to revitalize myself. I've watched Kate all day, and there's been no visible change. Dad's checked on her twice. I couldn't read his expression, but Tammy's? Tammy is an open book.

Two hours ago, she came in. Her bottom lip set between her teeth, she scanned over every single read-out the machines gave up. She took Kate's blood pressure twice.

When she was satisfied, she sighed. "Well, we have twenty-four hours left."

"What does that mean?" I'd asked.

She hesitated. "Twenty-four hours is a long time. A lot can change."

Since Marcy wasn't around at the time, Tammy didn't elaborate. Stupid privacy mumbo jumbo.

I drop to the floor and do fifty push-ups. I have to do something. It gets my blood moving a little. Enough to give my body the delusion that I've had some rest.

As I wait for my coffee, I sit on the bed beside Kate and stroke her arm. I've touched her so much in the last week that I can't imagine going a day without the skin-on-skin contact. Somewhere inside her, I hope she's gotten as much out of my caresses as I have.

I lean forward and press my mouth on hers. It's not the same when she doesn't kiss me back, but as soon as she does, I don't plan on letting her come up for air.

"Wake up and kiss me, baby," I say against her lips.

I pull back to gaze at her, and immediately her eyelashes flutter. This time, I don't hesitate. I know what I saw.

"Katie?" I breathe out. "Katie, can you hear

me?"

I study her in anticipation. But like earlier, nothing happens.

I can't take this much longer. She needs to fucking wake up!

After

At one in the morning, Marcy snores softly in the other bed, and I can't stay awake any longer. The coffee she brought me earlier wore off an hour ago. Even another set of push-ups didn't cut it.

I rest my head on my arms on top of Kate's blankets. The white noise of the machines lolls me, because that's what it has become after eight days. White noise.

My eyelids drop as I tick off another hour.

A hand skims over my hair. Her light, airy touch electrifies me, and suddenly, I'm awake. Wide awake.

I take in her eyes gazing back at me. Beautiful brown irises that put nature to shame. For a second, I wonder if I'm still asleep. But then she smiles at me. *Me.* The guy who came so close to walking away from her because he was too chickenshit to deal with his own insecurities.

These last eight days, I didn't keep coming back to her because of me. *I* haven't been holding onto her. No, she's been holding onto me.

"Hey there," I whisper.

I'm grinning like an idiot now as I scoot my chair closer to her. I never did come up with what to say to her. It's a good thing, though, because there are no words to express how I feel. A strange concoction of fear, elation, and inadequacy rises in my chest, and I can feel the sting in my eyes as I attempt to hold back my relief.

She's awake. She's okay.

Her eyelids close, and I can't let that happen. No, no. She can't close them again, not after she just woke up.

I bend over her to press a kiss across her lips. She lightly sucks mine, and it feels so damn good. I pull back a little to look at her. Her eyes are open again, and she's smiling. Fucking *smiling* at me.

I can't take it. I need her.

I cup her face between my palms, holding on tighter, but I'm not letting her go. Crushing my mouth against hers, I'm desperate. This girl drives me crazy, and I want all of her.

She presses a hand on my chest and pushes me back. She's gasping for the air I've robbed her of. Her gaze pierces into me as she touches her fingertips to her lips. Hot damn, that's sexy.

"Sorry," I say, staring at her mouth and wishing I could kiss her again.

She searches the room as she catches her breath. "Uh, um," she pauses, her brows pinched together.

"I'm…in the hospital."

I'm not surprised she doesn't remember. After all, she was passed out when we brought her here.

"The virus took over your system, and, because of the chemo, your body couldn't fight it," I explain, trailing my fingers down her face. I can't stop touching her.

She seems to have her breathing under control now, so I dip down to steal another kiss. "You've been out for eight days," I say against her lips.

"Eight days?" she repeats, her eyes widening in surprise.

I nod, then motion toward Marcy. "Your mother has been sleeping in the empty bed over there."

Kate doesn't glance over. Her focus remains on me.

"And you?" Her voice cracks a little when she asks.

Oh fuck.

I take her face in my hands again and peer into her eyes. They glisten under the soft light above her. "There's no way I'd leave you," I say, because it's true.

The corner of her mouth tips up at my words, and she has me. I can't live without this girl.

She peeks over at her mother. Before she settled down, Marcy popped two Tylenol PMs, so she'll be out for a while. Like me, Kate's mother is low on sleep.

"Would you like me to wake her up?" I ask.

Kate shakes her head. "No, let her sleep."

"I think she'd want to see that you're awake." In fact, I know she would. I'll do whatever Kate wants, though I hope she'll tell me not to worry about it. I'm selfish, and I want this moment all to myself.

"I know. But I don't have the heart to wake her; she looks so peaceful."

Her answer doesn't surprise me. Kate's the opposite of me—selfless.

"You should probably get some sleep too," I say, thinking of her well-being.

The silly expression on Kate's face makes me chuckle. "Apparently, I've been asleep for eight days." A small giggle passes her lips, and the sound shoots straight to my chest.

This moment is better than I expected.

"Okay, but it's four in the morning," I point out. It's not like there's anything we can do at this hour.

Kate studies me for a second before she pats the mattress beside her. "If it's not too much to ask, can you just hold me?"

The way she asks creates a longing inside me that I don't know what to do with.

This girl. This beautiful, sick girl wants me. Not Liam. Not even someone *like* Liam. Me. Messed-up, broken, undeserving me.

I may never be the man she deserves, but maybe that's okay. Because maybe the man she deserves isn't the one she needs. And that man, the one she needs? Yeah, I can be him. I *am* him. For as long as she wants me.

I slide in beside her and pull her against me. I'm still scared. Afraid of how she moves me and how this might turn out. But I'm not walking away. I'm *in* this.

Pressing my lips to her temple, I revel in her.

With her, I'm alive for the first time since before Liam died. I *feel* again.

My scars heal with every kiss, every touch from Kate.

"It's never too much to ask," I say.

I don't know what I'm diving into, but two days later when she asks me the question I've asked myself over the last week, I finally have an answer.

Kate drops her gaze, her voice unsure. "Why me, Damian? I'm sick."

I lift her chin and stare into those stunning eyes of hers. The eyes I longed to see over those eight days. "Because you don't expect me to be someone I'm not," I tell her.

And for the first time in years, I don't either.

The End

Coming 2015
From Limitless Publishing

Love Always, Damian

By d. Nichole King

Chapter 1

Damian

The box under my bed taunts me. I ignore it. This year, I won't succumb to its cries on this day.

"Fuck this shit." I roll off my bed and search the dresser for my keys. Not there.

Where the hell did I put them?

I yank the door open and round the corner into the bathroom. Nothing but the usual.

Out in the living room, I throw the cushions off the sofa and check the chair and the coffee table. A handful of loose change, a couple of empty condom wrappers, three McDonald's French fries, and a ten-dollar bill, which I pocket. No keys.

"God damn it!"

I stomp into the kitchen and grab Dylan's motorcycle keys from the drawer. Dude never misplaces anything. Predictable bastard.

Apparently he heard me because when I get back to the living room, he's standing there.

I glance at him on my way past. "Borrowing

your motorcycle."

"What are you doing, Damian?"

Turning around, I dangle the keys in front his face. "Borrowing. Your. Motorcycle." I repeat it slowly, enunciating every word so maybe he gets it the second time.

"Last day of finals is tomorrow." My roommate is annoyed. "Look, bro, it's been four years since Ka—"

Suddenly, I have Dylan pinned to the wall, my hand around his throat. I squeeze hard enough to make him understand. "You're my best friend, man, but I don't need your psycho-babble bullshit again. Not today."

Dylan sighs and nods as best he can.

I take a step back, letting go of him. He rubs his neck, and I feel a small pang of guilt. Dude means well.

"I can't deal with this right now." I flip the keys into my palm and walk out the door.

I love the sound of Dylan's motorcycle when I rev it up. The noise drowns out everything, especially the shit in my head. Her memory hasn't faded, not even a little.

Speeding down the street, I don't think. The route is on autopilot in my brain.

I park in my usual spot and stuff the keys in my pocket. It's Tuesday night, so the parking lot is almost empty. Good thing, too, because tonight, I want to be alone.

Loud music assaults me as soon as I walk in. I don't even look around to see who's there. No need; everything I want is behind the counter.

"What'll it be, Damian?" Max asks.

"Tequila. Straight up," I say, pounding my fist twice on the wood.

"Sure thing, man."

I don't sit on a stool, and I don't wait. On my way to a booth in the corner, I shoot a quick glance at the guys playing pool. I recognize a couple of them from school. For them, tonight is about relaxing. For me, it's about forgetting.

I slide in, running my fingers through my hair. The way her dark eyes still pierce me guts me to the core. They'll always haunt me.

"Damian, my love, my final wish is for you to let me go."

I can't do it.

"Two tequila shots."

I almost jump out of my seat at the sound, but when I stare at the waitress, I realize the voice didn't belong to *her*. Of course she would never have said that. She hated me drinking.

I give the new girl a quick nod. She turns, and I down the first shot, watching the way her ass moves as she walks away.

Flipping the glass over, I send a wave to Max, then knock back the other one. He usually cuts me off at ten, and tonight, that won't take long. It won't be enough to drown her out of my head, but it might be enough to make the images fuzzy.

"Are you happy, Damian?"

I squeeze my lids shut. What the fuck kind of question is that? A knife stabs me through the heart, and I want to vomit.

I hear two more glasses hit the table in front of

me, forcing my eyes open. My gaze darts to the nametag on the waitress' t-shirt, just inches above her left nipple poking hard into the cotton. I lick my lips.

Cameron.

I guess she'll do.

"Another round," I say.

As I wait, my mind takes me back to that morning, and how she waited until sunrise to leave me. Maybe it was her way of reminding me.

"It's amazing, isn't it? No matter how dark it gets, the sun always rises and starts a new day. The darkness is forgotten."

God, I miss her so much. Everything about her.

Cameron sets two more shots on the table, and I don't look at her this time. I'm gonna need more alcohol for that.

I rub my face with my palms.

"I'll always be with you."

Fuck, no!

I jab my fists into the seat, pain racing through my knuckles. She fucking left me all alone! She's gone and I'm here. It's not fucking fair.

The sting of tears threatens, so I kill the shots, one right after the other. I slam the second glass on the table too hard, but I don't care.

When Cameron comes back over, she sets two more in front of me and says, "Rough night?"

I huff and down the first one. "You could say that."

Her bare thigh is so close to me. I can't wait to feel it up later.

"Bring me two more, if you would," I say.

She bites her lip. "Um, I don't know. Max…"

"Just bring me the fucking shots. Max and I have an agreement."

Cameron glances over her shoulder at the bartender. Getting the confirmation from Max, she swings around.

"I'll be right back."

I lean back, rubbing a finger over my lips, the alcohol finally kicking in.

"You have a whole life in front of you. Don't waste it. Don't dwell on the past."

Cameron saunters over with a tray of my last two shots of the night. I stare at her thighs, already imagining what they taste like. *I'm moving on, baby. Just like you told me to.*

"Thanks," I say as she sets them down. "When are you off?"

She hesitates. "Um, like, now. My boyfriend is picking me up."

Well, shit.

I down the last two and go up to pay my tab. My buzz was decent, but not enough. It's never enough anymore.

"Thanks, Max."

"See ya, man."

Stuffing my hands in my pockets, I take my time walking across the parking lot to Dylan's motorcycle. I pull out the keys and rev the engine. Her face isn't gone, but it's barely recognizable now. Just how I need it.

Slowly, I back out and notice Cameron standing against the side of the bar, hugging her arms from the chill.

Stood up. Sweet.

I pull up next to her. "Need a lift?"

"Uh, no. Toby should be here any minute."

Toby Stanton? Cameron might be an even better lay than I imagined.

"Toby should have been here by now." I reach my hand to her. "Come on. I'll take you home."

She bites her lip again, and I hope to know what that feels like in about ten minutes.

Cameron sighs and takes my hand. "I live on campus—Frederiksen Court."

I help her up behind me, her arms slipping around my waist. Smirking, I say, "Hang on."

We peel out into traffic, the wind slamming against my face. Cameron nestles her head into my back and holds me tighter. She says something, but I can't hear her.

On the way back to mine and Dylan's apartment—off-campus—I take a shortcut. By now, I just need to get Cameron naked. Fuck everything else.

I park beside my BMW and shut off the engine.

"I said Frederiksen Court," Cameron says, confused.

I climb off and get back on, facing her. "I said I'd take you home. This is where I live."

"Toby—"

"—is off fucking someone else and forgot about you." My hands find her knees and begin sliding up her thighs. They feel as good as they look.

She frowns, but doesn't say anything. I'm right, and she knows it.

Taking in every inch of her skin, I run my

fingers up her inner thighs as what I said sinks in. To let it go deeper, I kiss her neck, sucking on the flesh. She'll cave. They always do.

"He's probably working out late at the gym," she says, trying to convince herself.

"Yeah, probably not." I switch sides, and she tilts her head, letting me continue. Down below, I move her panties to the side to massage her. She stiffens a little, gasping.

"Toby…he's a…a National Champion boxer. He—uh—" She pauses, her breaths become shallow, just how I like it.

Yep. Toby Stanton. This is gonna be good.

She swallows. "He works out a lot."

I grunt. "I bet he does."

I know *he does.*

She nods. "He does."

Her hips start to move against my fingers, and I crush my lips into hers. I'm not surprised that she returns the kiss with fervor. Toby only gets the feisty ones.

My fingers start slipping on her, and I can't take it anymore. I've got to get my mouth on that.

When I let go, a disappointed gasp escapes her. I help her off the bike and lead her inside to my room. Thankfully, Dylan is already in bed. He hates when I bring girls home.

My shirt's over my head before I have the door closed behind me. Kicking it, it slams closed. I don't take the time to lock it.

Cameron fumbles with my belt; Fuck that shit. I pull her close, slide my hands under the waistband of her skirt, feeling every inch of the smooth skin.

Walking her backwards to my bed, I lean into her until she sits and I can finish the job, tossing the black wad and her panties across the room.

With her sitting there, I undo my belt and jeans, stepping out of them. Toby is clearly out of her thoughts now. She moans in excitement. Now to get the rest of her goddamn clothes off.

Gliding my palms up her thighs, I take a short detour between them.

"Oh, yes!" she cries out as I slip inside of her. I finger her until she's on the verge of coming.

Pulling out, I chuckle, knowing it's about to get a whole lot better real quick. She frowns, giving me puppy-dog eyes.

"Don't worry. I'll be back," I whisper in her ear.

She throws her head back with a smile on her face.

I grab the bottom of her shirt and begin to lift it, but it won't move past her chest. She'd pinned her nametag to her bra.

"Oh, Cameron," I groan. I hate that I have to take the extra time to undo the damn thing.

"Sorry," she says, panting. Music to my ears. "Here, let me get it." She turns the top of her shirt inside out, unhooking the pin. "There. Oh, and this is my friend's nametag. I forgot mine. My name is Katey."

Someone just punched me in the stomach.

'Don't leave me, Katie. I'm gonna fuck up, but don't leave me.'

"Get. The fuck. Out," I breathe.

Her brows furrow. "Excuse me?"

"Get the fuck. Out of here." I gather up her

clothes and shove them in her chest, knocking her backwards a little. "Now."

The pathetic look on her face doesn't faze me. She means absolutely nothing to me.

I throw the door open and don't look at her as she shuffles out undressed from the waist down. I don't give a shit.

"How am I supposed to get home?"

"I don't give a damn," I say and slam the door in her face.

A stunned second later, she screams, "You're a fucking asshole!" from the other side.

I collapse on the bed, my face buried in the blankets.

Yeah, Kate, I know. I know.

Acknowledgements

This novella tested me. Written all in Damian's point of view, I had to dig deep. Being inside his head isn't the greatest place to be. But I think Damian is all of us. In some way, we're all broken, and we're all searching for that miracle that will put us back together. We're all looking for peace.

I could write a whole novella of thank-yous and still, I wouldn't scratch the surface of my gratitude.

First, foremost, and always, I thank God, my Lord and Savior. Without Him, none of this would be possible.

Secondly, my family. My awesome husband who reads through all of my books and gives me his valuable insight, especially on the male psyche. My kids who have to put up with my scatterbrainedness and oftentimes late (or burnt) dinners. I love all of you so, so much.

To my extended family who have been incredibly supportive. I'm lucky to have you in my life.

Thank you to my CPs. Geez. I can't even tell you how thankful I am for you. Sunniva Dee and Laura Thalassa, I love your axes. I'm sure they're dipped in pure gold, and if they aren't, they should be. From line-by-line edits, to social media support, to work dates, to late night chats about Disney princes and princesses—oh, and let's not forget about Mr. Frumps!—I appreciate everything. <3

For my beta readers: Tonille Burrows, Temperance Elisabeth, Kim Jackson, and Heather Jelsma. Your input is greatly valued. From the depths of my heart, thank you!

To my street team. Thanks for being there for me. Thanks for loving my books. Thanks for your opinions. Thanks for promoting my books. Thanks for the amazing teasers. Thanks for a whole list of stuff that's too long to mention here. Just, thanks!

A huge shout out to the bloggers and reviewers who have supported me and this series. I'm too scared to name you all because I'll probably leave someone out, but you know who you are. You've helped get my name out there, loved my books, and welcomed me into the writing community with open arms. You deserve so much more than a simple "thank you." Really, you do.

Toni Rakesaw, my editor, you have been a joy to work with. You mention things that never crossed my mind, and you catch my embarrassing counting errors. One shot, two shots, three shots... ☺ Seriously, thank you!

Eden Crane Designs. Another beautiful, beautiful cover. I can't wait to see what you come up with next!

Eternal thanks to Limitless Publishing! Jennifer O'Neill, Jessica Gunhamer, Dixie Matthews, thank you!! Thank you!! Thank you!! It's been a pleasure.

And finally, to the readers. This book, especially, was spawned because of you, your comments, your emails, your reviews. When I wrote *Love Always, Kate* this novella wasn't even a blip on my radar. You wanted it, so I wrote it, and I hope you love it. This book is for you.

Love Always, d.

About the Author

Born and raised in Iowa, d. Nichole King writes her stories close to home. There's nothing like small-town Midwest scenery to create the perfect backdrop for an amazing tale.

She wrote her first book in junior high and loved every second of it. However, she couldn't bring herself to share her passion with anyone. She packed it away until one day, with the encouragement of her husband, she sat down at the computer and began to type. Now, she can't stop.

When not writing, d. is usually curled up with a book, scrapbooking, or doing yet another load of laundry.

Along with her incredible husband, she lives in small-town Iowa with her four adorable children and their dog, Peaches.

Facebook:
www.facebook.com/dnichole.king

Twitter:
https://twitter.com/dNicholeKing

Website:
www.dnicholeking.com/

Pinterest:
www.pinterest.com/dnicholek/

Goodreads:
www.goodreads.com/author/show/7762889.D_Nichole_King